Cas

Emma Cavendish

Copyright © Emma Cavendish, 2025
All rights reserved. No part of this book may be reproduced or distributed in any form without prior written permission from the author, except as permitted by UK copyright law.

This book is a work of fiction.
Names, characters, places and incidents are either a product of the author's imagination or are used factiously. Any resemblance to actual people living or dead, events of locales is entirely coincidental.

A love letter to my friends, who always make space for the things I cannot say.

And a reflection, on all the things I wish he would say.

Everything is copy
Nora Efron

Chapter 1. Her.

I don't really get the 'hamster on the wheel' feeling. I understand the metaphor but if you think about it, you could just step off the wheel at any moment. I feel more like I'm hungover at a fun fair. It looks like I'm having a blast, but I'm one rollercoaster away from throwing up and lying down behind a bin.

Okay, maybe this is a bit melodramatic. Going back to three days in the office is giving me too much time to think on my drive to work, and there isn't enough new music to distract me.

I'm driving to Hitchin, a place you only know if you live there, have passed it on the slow train from Cambridge, or know someone who works at Central Distribution Ltd, the second biggest logistics company in the UK. If you do, there's a good chance I'll know them. Not because I'm a total socialite, but because I've been working there for six years in four departments, so you could say I've been around. Arguably both in and out of work, but let's not go down that road right now.

I love my job, but I also have a habit of saying that when I'm actually stressed and overwhelmed. There's a fine line between being a high-performing perfectionist and being burnt out, and unfortunately, I hopscotch between those lines on a weekly basis.

I frequently find myself muttering, 'I love my job, I love my job, I love my job' during the day like a desperate first assistant at Runway magazine. Either that or whispering 'you better fix me' aggressively to my morning coffee. If someone secretly miked me up for a day in the life at work, they would probably be pretty concerned about my mental health.

It's Thursday morning in the office, and by 9:30am I'm power walking to find a meeting room after finishing my first two calls. The call is already halfway through, so I open the door slowly, doing the universal silent wave and awkward closed mouth smile of a late apology, and sit down between one of my team and a couple of new faces.

My manager asked me, or 'told me' may be more accurate, to cover an operations role temporarily last year, and after a few months I decided to stay as a development opportunity. It's completely different from my previous roles in strategy, but I love learning so it's great to be challenged in a new way – even if it's also consistently the most frustrating job I've ever had in my life.

The meeting wraps up quickly, and I only have to suppress a mild urge to throw my laptop at a colleague, before we take the next steps and finish a few minutes early. Giving me time to walk, instead of run, to the next session.

Jumping into complicated problems is exactly what makes my job so interesting. It's really cool getting to have such a big impact, but it's a double-edged sword because I see everyday what would happen if I didn't make the effort I do.

The trouble is, after a day of back to back meetings, I'm so tired I have to, as my friend Dani would say, 'drag my re-animated corpse around' if I want to do anything else.

The rest of the day goes pretty smoothly so I'm feeling sufficiently fine as I drive home. So fine I can listen to normal music instead of blazing the Beastie Boys at full volume to scream 'Sabotage' all the way down the A1.

By the time I get home I'm happily towards the intermission of *Hadestown* and ready for normal conversation that doesn't involve taking things offline, next steps, or stakeholder management.

"Hiya!" I call out cheerfully as I step into the flat, feeling a burst of energy that never fades when I see May, my flatmate. After a long day, this enthusiastic greeting is my signature way of announcing my arrival. We've been best friends since we were thirteen, capturing our lives with digital cameras in the park, and it feels like coming home every time I walk through the door.

I'm incredibly lucky that May wanted to move to this flat last year and invited me to take the second bedroom. She and her mum debate over who masterminded my move, but whoever it was I'm grateful. The flat is a spacious two-bedroom with large glass windows and a balcony overlooking Regent's Canal. The open-plan kitchen and lounge are a Londoner's dream, but the view is my favourite part. The low residential buildings across the canal give an open view of the sky, which is incredibly therapeutic after a busy day navigating the city.

I wouldn't trade city life for anything, but bustling around the narrow streets can leave you feeling like a lost mouse sometimes. Or a hamster, if you will.

"Hiiii!" she responds, popping her head around from the kitchen as I kick off my boots and drop my bags.

"How was your day?" I ask, stepping into the kitchen.

I head to the fridge and grab my ready-meal carbonara, popping it into the microwave. I usually love meal prepping, but when work gets hectic, it's the first thing to fall by the wayside.

"My day was good, thanks! Henry was in today and started sharing his views on dating again, which was… interesting," May says, her eyes sparkling as she ties her long blond curls up into a bun. Henry is her latest work crush, one of many. May firmly believes, in the words of Billie Eilish, that "if you don't have a crush, then what's even the point of living".

She also believes all men, or potential romantic prospects,

should start in jail. Hypothetical Monopoly board jail that is, or something similar. They have to earn their way into your heart through strong positive actions, not mediocrity and the bare minimum. This doesn't necessarily apply to crushes, who can continue as questionable prospects as long as they provide entertainment. Henry being a case in point.

"What were his most interesting views?" I ask, curiously.

"He thinks you shouldn't sleep with a girl until the third date, otherwise, you'll lose interest." May's tone is laced with scepticism as she begins to tidy up her work-from-home setup at the kitchen table.

"Charming," I reply. This is one of those views that inherently feels wrong but takes a minute to work out why. May and I are always open for debates but I can't help but hold back when it's about someone else, just in case there's an accidental invisible line that may be crossed.

"Thoughts?" she prompts, her laptop paused mid-air.

I carefully extract my meal from the microwave, pouring it into a bowl and grabbing a fork, partly to buy time to think. "I kind of get it, but the idea of withholding sex to make someone get to know you seems tragic. It's like saying that waiting for sex is the only thing that will keep them spending time with you." I say, settling onto the sofa.

"Agreed. Plus, someone can lose interest at any point, so waiting doesn't really guarantee anything." May adds, her brow furrowed in thought.

"Exactly. I've been on dates where I've slept with someone

multiple times, or not at all, and still lost interest regardless." I say.

"It really comes down to the person and the connection, not just the timing of when you sleep together."

"Definitely." We delve into these everyday romantic dramas like experts, even though both of us have been single for over a year.

"But I can see why someone might hold off if they genuinely like someone," I continue, twirling my pasta thoughtfully. "If I like someone, I might hesitate to sleep with them out of fear of getting too attached, you know?"

"I thought you said if someone likes you, the sex doesn't matter?" May says, her laptop still in hand, a teasing glint in her eye.

"It shouldn't matter," I reply, "but when you have feelings for someone, you might worry they'll lose interest after you sleep together – the 'Henry approach' if you will. Especially if sleeping with them may make you like them more as it makes the connection more intense. It's unavoidably intimate." I pause, reflecting on a similar situation I faced earlier this year.

"But not as intimate as holding hands," May replies, flashing a playful smile as she turns back to the kitchen.

May is joking about my slightly controversial views on the "intimacy-physical contact spectrum". Sex is unavoidable physical intimacy, but it's only emotionally intimate if you like the person. One can have sex with someone one doesn't even like (or at least I can) with very little emotional investment.

Whereas, holding hands is the most intimate thing you can do with someone because it's so emotionally intense, even if less physically so. Holding someone's hand is a public declaration that you're intertwined, that you're a couple. It's a way of telling your partner what they mean to you, in a steady, understated, yet romantic way. It certainly feels like a lot of pressure to me, even when it's just a gentle touch.

I've only held hands with one person I've dated in the past year and when I told May had screamed in delighted surprise. That was the same person I was afraid to sleep with because I liked them so much. Despite waiting until the fourth date out of nerves, they still lost interest one date later and it ended shortly after that. Not sure which argument that supports – that it's better to wait, or that they may lose interest regardless?

While May heats up her food, I instinctively open the dating apps with a fork full of carbonara paused in the air to cool down. Hinge. Bumble. Feeld. Her. If my life is like being hungover at a fun fair, then the dating section is the haunted house. Except all the underpaid actors dressed up as monsters are played by your exes. They wouldn't even need to dress up.

I can picture it now. The house could be set up for maximum impact by lining the exes up in order of emotional trauma. You're sold a ticket by that guy you dated at university who openly said he "doesn't really have any interests" (some people need to learn how to lie better). After being ushered through the door by the guy from work who said sitting on a bench side by side was "too intimate", you get your first jump scare from that Irish guy from Feeld you went out with in January. The one that was way too into rock climbing and bought you a glass of wine without asking what you wanted, whose name you don't remember but had an incredible six pack. The fear would only build as you ran fearfully past the blurred faces of all the people who ghosted you over the years.

When you think you're in the clear – the grand finale. You step into the daylight, then you realise it's a trap. A trick final room! You're locked in with your long-term international ex and he gaslights you into apologising to him for thinking he was lying (when he was), then tells you how you're dressed like a "classic English girl" who "wears really short things, you know, showing a lot of skin" before pushing you into a party full of all his cool edgy friends. The ex you were so in love with that you became completely colour blind to the countless red flags.

Thankfully London is big enough that the risk of bumping into an ex is unlikely – but never zero.

As per the normal routine, after messaging a few people per app, feeling completely uninspired and more drained than before – I put my phone down as May comes to join me on the sofa.

We rattle through our work days as we eat our dinners. I manically recount my most stressful and rewarding meetings, while May takes me through her friends' personal gossip. May works in marketing in an office full of 20-somethings new to London who love to socialise after work. Hence the spicy work crush conversation. In comparison, my spiciest work crush conversation involved teasing them for putting bold emphasis in all their emails.

"What are your plans this eve? Want to watch something?" May asks. We both love a chilled hang out together, but we also love our alone time. The assumption of most flatmates is just to put something on to watch, but in our flat it's a polite proposal in case one of us has important things to do – like having an everything shower and watching Friends in bed.

"Yes, I'm actually free. I can't face my inbox right now so let's just leave all that till tomorrow."

"Yey!" May cheers. She's always thrilled when I set a healthy boundary with work. I won't mention how I've made that decision by comfortably accepting I'll work this weekend instead. "Do you want to watch something new or…." She asks, picking up the remote.

"Definitely a rewatch night. I'm thinking musical, Les Mis?"

"Always – movie or 25th edition?"

"25th."

"Perfect, let's go."

Another important debate settled. What's the potential relevance of waiting to have sex on a date? And which version of Les Mis will we watch for an hour before going to bed? Just another busy Thursday evening as a wild 28 year old.

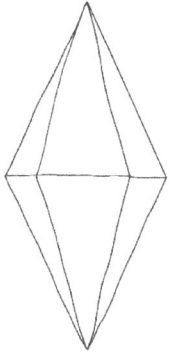

Chapter 2. Him.

Everyone says moving to a new city is so exciting. "Wow that's so cool!", "Man, I'm jealous!", "I've always wanted to live abroad." Yes, yes, very cool, very exciting. I am living the dream. However, it's also quite lonely. Super cool! And a bit lonely. The trouble is that making friends is hard. Meeting people is hard. And it turns out that as someone in their early 30s, everyone else my age seems to have already nailed this. Everyone has their group and regular hang outs. To be fair I had this too, but then I decided to "be brave and super cool!" and move to another city in another country. Which I will not let myself regret because I've always wanted to do this, I know I will be glad I did it. But right now it's not so much cool as awkward and lonely.

Thankfully I'm not completely alone. One of the reasons I wanted to move to London is that my best friend Leo lives here. He is definitely worth more than a whole group of mediocrity. The trouble is that when he is your only friend in the city, and he has been travelling for the past month and a half with his girlfriend – you start to think you'd settle for being in any group. Even one that is mediocre at best. It was very unfortunate timing that I moved here a few weeks before they left on their big trip.

I have been going into the office to try and make friends, but it hasn't been particularly successful. I work in a small company and it seems like everyone is on holiday just as I arrived. I spent almost all of Thursday sitting in silence at my desk and I wasn't even the only one in the office. There was a guy a few desks over but my attempts to start a conversation were aggressively shut down when he put on his headphones as I was mid-way through asking him about his weekend plans.

I'm trying to build some sense of community by starting a local routine for myself. I've gone to the same coffee shop round the corner from my flat in Brixton every Friday morning for the past month, which does create a sense of familiarity but also makes me feel like an NPC, or a Sim being played by a very unimaginative child.

That is where I'm currently sitting, reading my book, pretending not to be thinking about everyone noticing me. Are they wondering if I'm genuinely reading my book with my coffee, or am I sitting here performatively to seem cool and interesting? It's neither of those options, actually. The truth is, I'm just a bit lonely.

I'm also probably being far too self-absorbed. I don't think anyone is paying me any attention. Something I've noticed about London already is how active and anonymous it is. You can go, wear, and do anything – and everyone seems completely relaxed about it. Perhaps it's because London is such an international city. Sitting in the café, I can hear two languages I don't recognise being spoken at the tables nearby. With such a mix of people and cultures, you can sort of blend in however you like. It's comforting in a way because there's still an element of friendliness despite this anonymity. I've only been coming to this café for a few weeks, but the owner is already asking me about my week like I've lived here my whole life.

I have been pushed towards dating by my friends from home as a way to meet people or at least create some short-term company. But having only officially rejoined the dating scene a few months ago, I'm not sure I have the heart for it yet. I've never tried casual dating before, and I can't handle something serious right now.

It's hard enough being in a new city, let alone when you were meant to be here with your ex. I understand Karina's decision not to move away from her family, but I just wish she'd had the guts to tell me a year ago when we first agreed to move abroad together. Instead, she had waited until her masters finished, after I had already accepted a job in a new city. Ah well. We move on. Literally. I moved here and she moved out of our apartment into a flat share somewhere back in Berlin.

That may be why settling in has been so difficult. Not only am I lacking my usual friend support system, but I've lost my partner for the everyday conversation. I can always text other friends, or Leo, but it's not the same as having that one person on a different level who is just there for you, as you are for them. The one good thing about this intense break up is that being in a different country eliminates the temptation for a late night 'I miss you' or an invite for drinks. Yet it still feels strange and sad to not know what she's up to this weekend, or how her family is doing.

Thankfully this should be the final day of my weeks-long stretch of no serious friendship support and spiralling break up reflections. Leo is back tomorrow and we're going out for dinner. He is the sort of person to kindly introduce his friends to other friends, which might help me meet more people to hang out with.

In the meantime, it's just me and the *Silmarillion* passing the early morning surrounded by excitable 20 somethings and chai lattes.

Chapter 3. Her.

I wish I could sleep in. It feels like such a secret skill. I have plenty of secret flaws, like my inability to crack time differences or know the order of the seasons off the top of my head. But a secret skill I would love is to sleep in, or, even sleep more than 7 hours. I feel like after 10 hours sleep I would wake up a whole new woman, like when you forcibly 'End Task' when Excel crashes. Instead, I'm awake at 6:30am on a Saturday morning and feeling so restless I'm out of bed by 6:45.

I didn't have the heart to plan any dates with people I don't care about, so I had a free Friday night which led me to going to the gym at 8pm. Unleashing a sudden burst of energy on weights is better than sitting alone in the flat all night, or going on a truly last minute date which always brings out the poorest quality matches.

May was out with work friends at a birthday party last

night somewhere central and glamorous. I'm already eagerly awaiting the gossip that will follow. But as May has the magical gift of being able to sleep in past 6:30am, I'll have to wait until I see her later this morning for the debrief.

My Saturday morning agenda starts with a riding lesson. Getting back into riding wasn't something I had planned, but since starting a few months ago I don't know why it took me a decade to do it. I am a formerly closeted horse girl and will not apologise for it. 'Horse girl' shouldn't be an insult anyway, no one would say this about boys who love cars or football. What a surprise, it's an insult because it's for girls.

Once I've finished riding, my next agenda item is cleaning the flat and sorting some errands before going for dinner with Dani, one of my best friends. She is freshly back from a month and a half of travelling around Asia. Dani and I have been friends since sixth form and having her away for so long has been a tragedy for me on a macro scale.

She was about to begin a new job as a product manager at a tech start-up when she decided to push the start date back. Luckily, the company has a wonderful view on holidays and happily allowed it. It's just one perk of working in a start up with a great culture, which is a great fit for Dani as she's so adventurous and creative.

I assume everyone has secretly ranked preferences of their friends' partners, and within my ranking Dani's boyfriend is top of the charts. He and Dani have such a beautiful relationship it really sets the bar for me.

It also shines an inspirational light in the middle of my dating dark ages. While Dani was single, she treated dating like a part time job. She came up with the term 'Adminge' – referring to the daily admin required to get through your Hinge messages and matches. She is a firm believer that love doesn't just fall into your lap, you have to put yourself out there and find it.

I've taken the same approach in the past year, dating a real mix of people and giving everyone with potential at least a second, and normally a third, date just to be sure. Dani believes the fifth first date is where the gold dust lies, at least based on her experience. You meet four people with moderate potential, then the fifth person is something surprisingly magical.

She's either far better at picking her dates than me, or much luckier. So far this year, I've gone on at least three dates with six people. Yet I'm still spending my Friday nights doing weights at the gym listening to Spotify's shambolic 'British Work Out Hype' playlist.

Some quick mental maths tells me that means I've spent almost three weeks' worth of evenings dating people I no longer speak to, and it's only September. Those are the same people I don't want to be thinking about on my drive across London this beautiful Saturday morning. I need to refocus on the day ahead and think positively.

Being single in the depths of a long period of unsuccessful dating means you have to live in a permanent state of detached delusion. Detachment from the fact that this year I've dated people from apps, parties, friends of friends, work – and am still right where I started. With only a few more entertaining anecdotes and tearful nights to show for it.

Layer on a blanket of self-deprecating humour, and then cover it all up with a completely deluded optimism. Optimism that despite the inability to find the right loving relationship so far, the right person is just around the corner. Which means you should appreciate all the wasted dates and interesting characters you've met because you could be in the perfect relationship at any moment.

It's a lot to hold onto, so I'm grateful I won't be thinking about it for the next hour as I pull into the stables. Riding is an incredible distraction. I'll be too focussed on not looking like an absolute muppet trotting around, under the critical eye of a crowd of professional level 8-year-olds waiting for their jumping lessons.

Back at the flat after riding, May is up and enjoying her breakfast yoghurt on the balcony. I slide off my Birkenstocks (the perfect post riding boot slipper), grab a glass of water and step out to join her.

"Hey cowgirl," she greets me, making me smile inside and out.

"Hey buttercup," I welcome back.

"How was riding?"

"Delightfully difficult. I got stressed about the children and parents watching from the sidelines and accidentally steered the horse into a post." I say, feeling my already bruising knee.

"Classic mistake."

"Keeps me humble. How was the party? Any more controversial opinions?"

"No, but Annie and Jake got back together."

"No! Well Annie is going to regret that once Ben gets back from secondment." The delight of being invested in someone else's work drama, it's like watching a reality TV show.

"I know, something dramatic for the next work drinks, I'm sure. Remind me what's on the agenda for today?" she asks, putting down her finished yoghurt and moving onto her cup of tea. Lady Grey with a hearty helping of oat milk. There's something comforting about knowing someone's tea order. It's an everyday romance.

"Clean flat, shower, return parcels and then out for dins with Dani and Leo." I answer, chugging my glass of water. It's the second week of September but classic British weather has kept us guessing to the last minute, meaning this has been a bizarrely warm day and I had sweat through my jeans and boots during my lesson within the first few laps.

"Ah yes, I forgot they're back now! Where are you heading for dinner?"

"Flour & Grape in London Bridge I think?"

"Delightful. Give them my love."

"Of course. What about you popcorn?" I say.

"Brunch with the work girlies – to debrief last night. Then Bethan is coming over for dinner on the high street somewhere. So, we might come back for a movie or go out for drinks. We'll have to check the vibe." May lists off, still cradling her tea.

"It's always one or the other. Please give the girlies my love. Feels like both of those could tip into drinking so could be a big boozy day for you at this rate."

May leans back with her arms out like some kind of boxer trying to face off. "Sorry I can't help being a massive lad?"

"That would be more convincing without the Emma Bridgewater pigeon mug in your hand." I say, pushing myself up to move back into the kitchen.

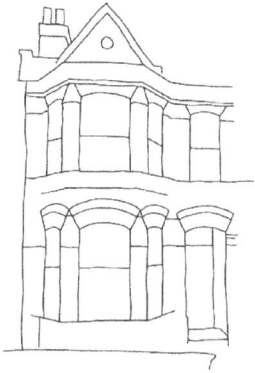

Chapter 4. Him.

Having no friends in the city is doing wonders for my sleep schedule. Last night was very adventurous. After my big morning coffee trip, I spent most of the day working from home in the flat. Given the lack of a social scene in the office, it doesn't provide me with a big motivation to go in every day.

Once I was done with work, I spent a few hours making an extremely complicated Ottolenghi mushroom lasagne to pass the time, then watched a documentary on the Space Shuttle Challenger until bedtime. I'm not a big party animal at the best of times, but I would be open to a slightly more energised Friday night.

Waking up on Saturday morning I feel rested and ready for the day, which is slightly bittersweet given that I also have very little to do this morning. I'm going to work this afternoon, but I am essentially waiting to see Leo. It's unusual for me to be craving social company so strongly, or at all. I'm quite introverted, but not having any close friends to talk to or spend time with in the past month is an extreme end of the spectrum even for me. I am starting to build a good friendship with my flatmate, but she's been away a lot recently so it's still a work in progress.

I'm almost unreasonably excited about seeing Leo and Dani this evening. I feel like I'm 22 again, patiently queueing up for the latest *Elder Scrolls* game to be released.

Unlocking my phone in bed I realise it's only 9am. There are still a few hours before I need to head out. I weigh up the options for the morning – go back to the coffee shop to read, stay in bed, watch TV, make a decadently big breakfast, or exercise? Exercising feels like the best choice. It's strangely warm in London despite it being September, and somehow not yet raining today, so it will be nice to get outside.

The flat I'm renting is between Brixton and Clapham, which means I'm lucky enough to have parks within a short run on each side. I get myself ready to go and decide to head towards Brockwell Park. I don't have an exercise routine, I tend to make time for it when it suits me and while I'm always down to try a new sport or activity, running is my favourite. It makes me feel like part of the neighbourhood being out amongst the rest of the locals. It's something I've always loved but has become especially important since moving.

Running through Brixton I can see the regular eclectic mix of people already bustling around the station and shops. In the five minutes it takes for me to run past, I clock incense burning, missionaries, fresh produce for sale, what looks like human rights campaigners, and a busker. I've already started to appreciate how diverse London is, but Brixton is on another level. It's like an intense microcosm of every kind of person, bundled into a square mile, with a thousand shops and bars squashed in between. Making my way towards Herne Hill the streets become quieter and more residential, fewer campaigners and more cockapoos.

Brockwell is my favourite London park I've found so far. The sports fields and playgrounds create a real community feeling. There's something so comforting about seeing families out together, and friends walking with their morning coffees. It also provides a great view across London as a reward for running up the hill. Checking my watch, I decide to loop back to give myself time to shower and grab some breakfast, leaving a good buffer for my journey to work.

I may have just about worked out the running loop to Brockwell, but I still find myself getting extremely confused on the tube. I often give myself a bit of extra time in case I get lost. The feeling of anonymity is strongest on the tube where no one seems to want to look at each other. It may feel freeing in the cafes, but it feels cold underground. It's like eye contact is a cardinal sin within the confines of these metal cylinders. I try to fit in with the crowd and stick to looking at my phone in between stops. I recently discovered you can download the entire Wikipedia catalogue which provides endless entertainment on unexpected topics.

After the Challenger documentary I'm going down a black hole of space related content to keep me busy.

Working on a Saturday may seem like an inconvenience,

but when you don't have many friends, it works out quite well.

I work as a buyer for a small wine company. Working at the weekends isn't a normal part of the job, but we take it in turns being front of house in the shop to have the expertise available for customers. It's quite nice doing a customer facing role for a bit, getting to know the patrons of central London. Well, the patrons of South Kensington who are buying specialist wine – arguably not the average Londoner.

After putting my bag away, I settle in behind the counter and start tidying up the display. A few excellent white Rioja's are on the corner of the table, making me think of the remarkable Serrano ham I sampled when I first tried this grape in Spain. People think a good charcuterie means the most expensive wines and meats you can find, but it's about pairing quality goods from the same local area. Spanish ham, quince and honey, and a good Rioja makes for a great evening – just as well as a nice British beer with a sharp cheddar.

"Two weeks in a row?"

"Pardon?" I look up from straightening the lines of bottles to see the other employee, who had just walked in, looking at me expectantly. He's similar height to me, but younger, blonde and with an accent twang I can't place.

"You're here on a Saturday two weeks in a row? It's just unusual for the buyers, I always thought this was the worst part of the job for you guys. Who did you piss off?" he asks, laughing loudly. Not really appropriate language to use on the shop floor, but I don't have the heart to try and challenge this as a newbie.

"Actually the opposite, someone in my team is on holiday so I said I'd cover. I'm new to town so don't mind giving up a Saturday I would otherwise spend by myself." I laugh this off to try and make this sound less tragic, stepping away from the counter to the displays on the shelves. I can see a Vermentino tucked away that deserves a more prominent spot. It's the perfect balance of citrus sweet and the bitterness of grapefruit.

"Ah got you – very generous of you. I'm Tom by the way," he says, holding out a hand to shake over the neatly displayed rows of wine.

"Ryan."

"Nice to meet you Ryan – new to London, generous, with no friends. If you want some better Saturday company another week after work we should get a pint. There are a few class places for a piss up in the area."

"That would be nice, yeah," I say, actually thinking that doesn't sound very nice at all but trying to be polite. I'm down for a pint but a 'piss up' sounds grim. But I also only have one other friend in the city at the moment, so I'm not sure I can pass up an opportunity to double my circle. I hand him my phone and he adds his number.

Before we can nail down any more plans, our next round of customers comes in to keep Tom and I busy until my shift is over. As well as keeping me busy, it was great getting to know the customers better, understanding what sort of flavour palettes the locals have and what sort of events they are catering for. I'm already starting to think of a few family-owned vineyards I don't think we sell yet that could be a great addition. Something exciting to start on Monday.

But first, quick tube back to Brixton. Time to shower and change out of my work clothes into something actually very similar, but marginally different – from light chinos and a white shirt, to dark chinos and a light blue shirt.

I'm off to meet Leo and Dani in another part of London I don't know. I haven't heard from Leo all day but he has already sent the time and place, so I put it into maps and head off.

Chapter 5. Her.

Despite my very light schedule, I still managed to be late getting ready to leave. This meant my mental plan of '20 minutes – decide outfit, get dressed, do hair and makeup' turned into '6 minutes - get dressed, grab makeup bag'. 20 minutes to do everything was already ambitious. I fell back on one of my default outfits of blue jeans, chunky black boots, black tank top and denim jacket. 'Tank top' may be a generous description for a minimal piece of fabric, but long sleeves would be a waste of the last moments of summer warmth.

I couldn't tell you how many first dates I've worn this outfit to in the past year. More than 10. Maybe 15. I might have been 'hot girl summer-ing' a little too hard. I have a bad habit of planning dates as a distraction when I'm stressed. Since the stress is almost always work-related, my dates inevitably end up being at the end of an overrunning workday, giving me less than 10 minutes to get changed and out the door. At least it's allowed me to finesse a default wardrobe for some quick last-minute dressing.

Arriving at the restaurant after doing my makeup on the bus, and accidentally smearing mascara on my hand and under my nail, I walk up to the beautifully cool looking hostess and ask for a table for three. Flour & Grape is the sort of place you can't book, but if you're happy to have a drink at the bar first you can normally be seated at a table within 30 minutes. It's an art securing a table within a reasonable time frame when you can't book, which I'm only willing to do when the food is particularly good.

After being politely told I'm on the wait list, I squeeze past the cosy tables and head to the bar. This feels like a good time to text and let them know I'm here, so I drop a "Hey! Asked for a table. Just waiting inside, can't wait to see you guys!" to Dani and settle in.

It's a classically busy Saturday spot in London. Lots of glamorous yuppies and dinks who are making me feel a little underdressed, enjoying the wonderful pasta and wine, squeezed in together to create a happy buzz of chatter. Checking my phone, I can see the message hasn't been delivered yet, meaning they are probably on the tube and will be at least 10 minutes. Time for a drink while I wait.

As the 'Grape' in the title may suggest, this place specialises in fancy wine paired with incredible pasta. Picking up the menu I remember I know four types of wine. I can't see any of them on here, prompting a very puzzled frown to take over my face. This turns into genuine concern when I'm faced with paying London cocktail prices for a wine I have no idea if I'm going to like if I choose poorly.

"Need a hand?" a low voice to my left asks politely.

Looking to the barstool next to me, I see an incredibly handsome man. Going to nice places like this in a big city means I'm accustomed to seeing handsome faces, but not normally up close or speaking to me. Luckily a job of high-pressure situations and an older brother with a long line of ridiculously good looking and cool friends has trained me perfectly for this moment.

"Sraybe." Fuck.

The handsome face frowns. Large dark brows knit together.

"Pardon?"

"Sorry, I meant – I meant, maybe, I mean sure. That would be great. Assuming you know something about wine? Or is it the blind leading the blind?" My original 'sure / maybe' must be put into the past as soon as possible by turning the focus on getting the beautiful man talking. I start to fiddle with one of my rings out of a nervous habit to calm myself down.

He smiles, so polite again. And so cute. The bar has soft low lighting but I can just about see a collection of freckles on his cheeks. "I know a little," he says, "Do you know what you like?"

'Your face' is the first thing that comes to mind, but I probably can't say that. "Something light, dry and sweet."

"Like a great summer's day," he says, looking back down at the menu, which is good so he doesn't see me blinking at him stupidly. Come on Anna, pull it together. Deep breath, shoulders back, sit up straight, calm your hands, and relax your face.

"I would say the Riesling – it's light and a little sweet. Plus, it's from a really beautiful part of Germany which I always think helps the flavour."

"Okay I'm sold," I say, putting up a hand to flag down the bartender. "Can I get you something as a thank you?"

My assumption with all beautiful people is that they are in a relationship. They are married, living with their partner, parent of three, two small dogs – that sort of thing. I find it makes it easier to talk to them when you've accepted that you're not a potential romantic partner, and that they are just being nice to you as a friend. It removes the emotional investment or risk. May says this is called 'avoidant attachment', but I think it's just practical.

The last nice and handsome guy I asked out in person said yes, then followed up to say no because he was in a relationship. He just didn't know what to say because he was so hot and bothered. Not just because of me to be clear. We were in a sauna.

We started chatting with some classic sauna small talk ('did you know basically all houses in Sweden are built with saunas?' etc.), then he asked my name and kept the conversation going which felt like a sign of interest. I should have trusted my instincts – nice handsome people are already in relationships.

Another crowd-pleasing anecdote that one. Something about the novelty of the sauna seems to really tickle people.

Putting this handsome man in the 'married with a cat' bucket means I immediately feel calmer and more composed. It's a normal interaction with no potential crying inducing romantic drama on the cards. Which means I can keep appreciating his gorgeous face and friendly conversation, just with a steady heartbeat.

"I'm waiting for someone, but I'll happily start on Riesling," the handsome man says. There we go, waiting for someone of course. It looks like I am making a new friend while I wait.

"Least I can do." I say, ordering two glasses from the bar. "So, how is it you know this wine is so good?"

"I actually work in the wine industry, it's sort of my job to know what's good," he says, picking up his glass and holding it up to me with a "Cheers."

"Cheers" I say, gently clinking my glass to his, holding his eye contact as we take a sip. A good habit in general, but in this moment it's a great excuse to look into his eyes and appreciate the dark rich shade of brown looking back at me.

"Working in wine, what does that mean beyond professionally drinking? Which by the way you must do well because you're right this is delicious," I say, putting the glass down and starting to fiddle with my necklace.

He laughs, looking to the side slightly, prompting my eyes to glance at his neck. It's covered in dark stubble poking out of his light collared shirt. Goodness.

"It is a bit of professional drinking I guess, but in small quantities and with a lot of careful thought with each glass. I'm a buyer for a wine shop so I have to find new wines and build relationships to get the best merchandise. It's fun because there's always lots to learn, new vineyards, new businesses, new types of grapes." He takes another sip and I smile back at him, encouraging him to continue. "You get to work with the businesses closely so you really help them shape their trade. Like there's a vineyard in Italy that's started growing their vines in a different layout on the hills. It has completely changed the flavour profiles because of the different distribution of the sun on the grapes."

There's always a glow when someone is talking about something they really love and find fascinating, and this guy is absolutely radiant right now.

"That sounds really cool," I say. He looks sceptical, which makes me laugh. "No really! It's amazing how a lot of small changes can come together for such a big impact, and it must be cool working on something so tangible as well. You get to actually taste and experience the product of your work."

He smiles at me, "That's true, nice way to think about it. It sounds better than 'professional drinker' at least."

I laugh, sipping more of my wine. It's so delicious that I've almost finished. "Yes, but that's a cooler thing to put on your business card. Or a terrible stag-do t-shirt or something," which elicits a gorgeous rumbling laugh back at me.

"Yeah – sraybe." He says, his eyes sparkling up at me in the soft light, almost making me spit out my wine as I let out a very unladylike cackle of laughter.

I'm about to call out his unexpected roast but at this point both of our phones buzz, making us look down at our respective laps to read the updates.

I see a message from Dani, "I'm so sorry. Our flight was diverted via Iceland due to some engine issues and we had no service! Have just landed in Heathrow now so will have to miss dinner. So sorry for the late notice but would love to see you tomorrow if you're free? Xxx". I reply quickly saying no worries and suggest lunch tomorrow. With a newly free evening I could text one of the Feeld roster for a late night pick me up. But the prospect of such cold company immediately fills me with a wave of loneliness. It seems going home alone and getting an early night may be the more sensible option.

Looking up, I see the handsome man texting on his phone.

"I'm going to head off," I say, looking for the waiter again so I can grab the cheque.

"Oh okay, of course," he replies, looking up with a slightly surprised look. Maybe he was hoping I could keep him company until his partner (friend, husband, wife?) arrives. It is tempting, but I don't think I could handle seeing whatever gorgeous partner he has showing up to whisk him away.

The bartender comes with the bill, and just as I offer to pay, handsome man takes the receipt out of the bartender's hand. In the game of bill splitting Russian roulette, he's won this round.

"Hey, this was my treat as a thank you," I say, in my most politely commanding voice.

"Good company and good wine are my treat," he says back, tapping his phone against the card machine. Charming sentiment, but maybe too charming for a man in a relationship. He may just be being friendly but he's giving me butterflies.

I smile back, "Well thank you. It was lovely to meet you, enjoy your evening and wine!" I say, sliding off the stool. I walk out looking back down at my phone to find the bus.

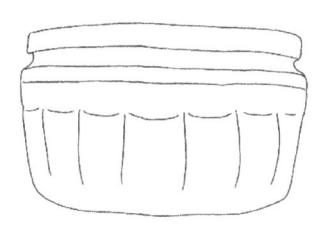

Chapter 6. Him.

Watching the mystery woman walk away I see a tattoo poking out of the back of her vest as she pulls on her jacket. It looks like a Greek bust of a woman. As I didn't have a chance to ask her anything about herself before she left, learning about her tattoos feels a bit ambitious. I'll have to leave that with the rest of the mystery.

Finishing off the last of my glass I can still picture her long dark hair and her grey blue eyes looking back at me. I've never struck up a conversation with a stranger before, apart from my recent failed attempts at bonding in the office. But watching her reading the menu was so entertaining it took me off guard. It was like she was trying to decipher the Da Vinci code, not pick a wine.

I also don't normally find it so easy to talk to strangers. Helping pick a wine is common practice for me. But something about her made me feel very comfortable beyond that. It felt familiar sitting and talking together. I'm not sure if it was the wine or the company but it also felt exciting. The way she held my eye contact as we drank, the way she always seemed to be moving or joking or laughing. It felt like something more exciting than making a new friend, maybe something more flirtatious.

My issue is that I don't have much practice with flirting so it's hard to tell. Karina and I were friends at Uni and I asked her out a few years later at a party. It was quite simple, everything happened so naturally. I've never tried to build a spark out of nothing, it's always just grown.

Given how quickly the mystery woman left, not even attempting to flirt was probably a sensible move. I clearly need more practice in talking to strangers full stop, and then converting that into friendship. At least this was good practice on the first point.

Re-reading the text from Leo about the flight delays, it seems like the only thing to do now is head home. After proposing a dinner on Wednesday via text to Leo, I finish the last sip of wine and follow the path of the mystery woman to head out.

As I step out my phone suddenly buzzes again. Instinctively, my heart jumps thinking that it may be a text from the woman – before I remember we didn't exchange numbers. Looking down I see a reply from Leo confirming dinner. I hover for a moment on Tom's name before changing my mind and going to Google Maps to find my way home. Enough drama for one day.

Stepping through the front door of my flat the sound of some extremely posh voices tells me that the show set in the fancy part of London is on, and my flatmate is home.

Taking off my shoes and walking into the lounge I see her and her boyfriend on the sofa. They have two of those tiny glass pot desserts they seem to love that taste like pure sugar.

"Hey you're back early, how was dinner?" Nicki asks. Nicki lives in the flat's other room and loves a lot of very British things that I don't seem to understand. I thought I knew a lot about British culture before moving here. I've seen all the *Harry Potter* movies – that's basically a documentary right?

"My friend's flight was delayed so we had to cancel. Is this the 'Murder in Mayfair' one?"

"*Made In Chelsea*," Nicki laughs back at me.

"But 'Murder in Mayfair' sounds sick, let's watch that!" her boyfriend Alex chimes in.

Alex lives out in the country somewhere, so he and Nicki spend a lot of weekends away with his family. They do kindly invite me along sometimes. But joining as a plus one on a family and couples weekend away doesn't feel like the right way to settle into London for me.

"Want to join? We have another pack of Gu desserts if you would like a Zillionaire Cheesecake?" Nicki offers, holding up another tiny glass pot.

"Thanks, but I'm not sure my German heart can handle that much sugar. Enjoy guys."

Their calls of goodnight follow me upstairs to the bathroom where I start brushing my teeth, still picturing the mystery woman from earlier. She just seemed very genuine, with this great energy. It was somehow the most comfortable conversation I've had with anyone, apart from Leo and Dani, since moving here. Even though we don't even know each other. How do I find nice people like that to befriend (or, you know, date) in the future?

Reading in bed I find myself getting distracted thinking about the way her hands wrapped around her necklace as she spoke. Whoever she rushed off to, I hope they had a great night because I feel like I could've done a good job of entertaining her if she'd only wanted to stay.

Chapter 7. Her.

"You're engaged!" I scream like a madwoman, tears already starting to form in my eyes. "Oh my goodness, you're engaged!" I scream again. Pausing to breathe I start crying fully, it's like when I saw Taylor Swift appear at the start of her Eras tour.

Dani is beaming at me, looking bashfully thrilled and doing a tiny version of the happy dance she normally reserves for when she eats really good food. I am, in comparison, causing a total scene, causing Dani's kind brown eyes to change from joy to concern.

"Okay Anna, it's alright, take a moment." She laughs, casually shaking back her cropped black hair as she pats me on the arm, her normal excitable yet composed self. Her light linen dungarees fit in perfectly with the soft woods and pinks on the walls around us.

We're in the cosy café nestled at the base of my building.

This beautifully serene space is adorned with plants, books, and a variety of dairy-free milk cartons. The proximity of their incredible baked goods is particularly tempting, and I've already accumulated several stamped cards worth of free coffees since moving here. I like to think of my frequent coffee and cookie stops as a way to support the local community – and to keep up with the latest additions to their polaroid collection of visiting dogs.

It's also the perfect spot to take a friend for brunch when they're kind enough to come to your side of town. Especially when they have such exciting news.

One of your best friends getting engaged is always a cause for celebration and emotion. This is my first best friend to get engaged, so it's hitting extra hard, especially because some of Dani's other familial relationships have been quite difficult. She had a really tough time during sixth form and spent many nights at mine for light relief and a safe space to crash. She's returned the favour a million times over by creating a safe space for me with her presence every time I see her.

She has also had her fair share of mediocre boyfriends. The ones that chip away at you until you become a diminished version of yourself.

Her relationship with Leo is nothing like that. He helps make her the best, biggest version of herself, which she tells me is what a relationship should do. Seeing her creating this amazing life, being so happy with this wonderful man, is enough to make anyone cry. Let alone a serial weeper like me.

However, my noise sobs are starting to become embarrassing, so I try to stop the train of thought of how much she deserves this and pull myself together. Dani helps by grabbing some tissues out of her rucksack and passing them to me.

"Sorry," I eventually get out, "I am just so happy for you."

"Oh really? I couldn't tell. I thought this was a response of pure unadulterated rage." Dani beams back at me sarcastically, prompting a watery chuckle. "But thanks, I'm pretty happy myself."

"This is unbelievable, I was expecting incredible updates from your travels around East Asia and then you land me with this as well. You have to tell me everything please – I want audiobook level detail. I want Tolkien-esque level slow." I say seriously.

"It was just towards the end of the trip. We'd left Laos and were spending a few days in Vietnam. We went to one of those places in Hoi An where you can get custom clothes made. Leo had been saying we should get something fancy made – something for a really nice dinner. So, he had a suit made and I got a dress."

"Wait – please show me pictures. Painting a picture with your words isn't enough, I need more." I interrupt.

Dani laughs as she gets out her phone and brings up a picture of her and Leo standing together in the shop. Leo in a plaid suit (classically bold choice) and Dani in a flowy teal dress.

"Babe, you look like a beautiful mermaid." I say.

"Thank you, that was the goal. So, we had the clothes made, and then Leo had booked a really nice dinner. It was incredible, I was happy dancing non-stop. And just when I thought it couldn't get any better, he proposed. You know Anna, it was really nice. He said all these lovely things and I was so overwhelmed that I had to get him to say his speech again when we got home." Dani says happily, with a soppy smile on her face.

"This is giving me the most enormous glow of joy inside. It sounds perfect." I say, smiling back.

"And I have a favour to ask as well," Dani says looking me dead in the eye, very seriously, over her tea.

"Of course, anything."

"We're not doing a big wedding party but, will you be my Maid of Honour?" Dani asks.

"Dude it would be my absolute pleasure and honour to be so. I will take this as seriously as Shang took the training of troops to fight the Huns in *Mulan*." I say, trying to hold back the tears again.

"Well good, because to handle this task properly you must be as swift as the coursing river." Dani says.

"You know I've heard that before somewhere – a classic bridal wives' tale, I think." I say, drinking the dregs of my cappuccino to keep me calm (as caffeine is known to do).

"Okay so that's my big highlight – what's going on in your world? Get me up to speed on channel Anna," Dani says expectantly.

This is difficult because when work is a drain on your physical, emotional and mental resources sometimes it's also all you can talk about. To avoid doing this, I jump to the other 'Anna specific' topic of dating. The secondary 'Anna specific' topic list would include hobbies, friends and family updates, and travel.

"I have been finding the dating apps are filling me with more dread than usual. So, I'm on the fence about either dating slightly terrible people that I know will have zero romantic potential, or not dating at all. The latter of which is probably more responsible but a lot less fun," I say, trying not to have too mournful an expression. It seems such a shame to be bringing the mood down, but I honestly don't know what else to say and I can't lie to Dani.

Dani nods sagely, "I can see that. Less fun but maybe more sensible. No good dates lately then?"

"I had a good one with a girl a couple of weeks ago, but I cancelled our second one. I was so tired from work and haven't had the heart to reschedule yet. I'm that guy we hate who does that after a great date and you think 'Why would he do that? How busy can work be?' But sadly, it's true. It's me. I'm the problem. I'm the fuck boy," I say sipping my water.

"Well, you know it's nice to see you branching out and trying something new. But I'm thinking it may be better to pause dating if you're feeling like that. I'm sorry it's filling you with dread." Dani says.

"It just feels a bit hopeless. I've dated a lot this year with no success. You know, I'm a data driven decision maker and right now, statistically, it feels like it's not going to work out – so why bother?" I say sadly, weaving punchline and honest fear together to soften the blow.

"Not sure I completely agree with the logic, but I get that you need to be in the right headspace to date – so taking a break might help." Dani says softly. "And avoiding more fuck boy level behaviour. I'm happy to start loading on Maid of Honour duties instead?"

"I can't think of anything that would bring me more joy." I'm already feeling happier about this better use of my time.

"Well, your first Maid of Honour duty is to form an allegiance with the Best Man as you guys will probably be managing the forces together. Are you free for dinner on Wednesday? It's one of Leo's friends from home and he's coming over so it could be a nice time to bond."

"Of course! I am so ready – one of my key skills at work is relationship building. This guy is going to love me."

Chapter 8. Him.

"Congratulations man! That's amazing!" I say, muffled into Leo's shoulder as we move out of our hug. I'm not normally a hugger, but your best friend getting engaged is a good reason to break the habit. We're in his apartment with his girlfriend – wait no, fiancée – Dani, and they both look equally thrilled as they beam at each other. The content smiles shared by two people deeply in love. For a second, I can picture Karina looking at me when we were together, completely in love and thinking about our future. I thought we would be getting married soon. Moving out of Berlin was meant to be the first step in setting up the next stage of our life together.

"So, you're my Best Man, right?" Leo asks, holding out the plates as we resume laying the table, pulling me away from my thoughts.

We're in their kitchen, which seamlessly opens onto the

living room, with a dining table perfectly positioned in the middle. The walls are adorned with art ranging from the poetic to the ludicrous – like the print of mountains on one side of the window, and the cross-stitch 'Live – Love – Lobotomy' on the other. Various plants are scattered across every surface, creating a warm and grounded atmosphere.

I always knew Leo was a big fan of cooking, and it seems he's found a great partner in Dani. She is just as enthusiastic about good food – handmaking ravioli for dinner tonight. As Leo and I lay the table, Dani juggles several pans on the hob, all while dancing slightly on her toes to the Wet Leg album playing in the background.

"Of course, dude, it would be an honour. I didn't move all the way here to just sit in the crowd." I say, setting down three plates. "You gave me an extra." I add, holding the plate back up to Leo.

"My friend Anna is joining us for dinner." Dani says, as the frying pancetta and butter emits heavenly smells. "We meant to introduce you guys on Saturday but sadly British Airways had other plans. I thought you two might get on anyway, but she's also my Maid of Honour, so the meeting is extra important now."

"Right, so she's the competition?" I ask jokingly, setting the plate back down on the table.

"More like a partner in crime." Leo replies, adding cutlery and glasses to the table.

"I'm not sure – it feels like we've got two rival parties going on here, the bride and groom?" I shoot back, leaning against the chair and taking a sip of my beer.

"Yes, weddings are famously about rivalries – not like, the coming together of families in matrimony, and love and stuff."

The intercom buzzer rings, and Dani jumps over and answers hello, letting the newcomer up. I noticed Dani's infectious energy the minute I met her, she's the sort of person to physically jump with joy. Her open enthusiasm pairs nicely with Leo's quiet calm.

"Anything I should know about this Anna person?" I ask, in a joking way but with a mildly serious undertone. I'm happy to meet new people in theory, but it's always a bit nerve wracking, especially when they're already connected to people you know.

"Anna's great. Really friendly. High energy, although maybe that's work dependent," Leo replies, bringing over the cheese on a plate with the grater – always a happy sight.

The door opens with a friendly call of "Hiya!" and in steps a familiar tall, elegant frame with long dark hair in wide leg stripy trousers. Mystery woman. Mystery solved. Anna.

Anna goes in for a hug with Leo straight away and then looks over to the kitchen to wave to Dani as she takes off her trainers before spotting me. "Hi?" She looks at me questioningly while tilting her head. Then a happy warm expression comes on her face as Leo steps back and introduces me.

"This is Ryan, my friend from home – and Best Man."

"The wedding squad is here!" Dani shouts from the hob, making a celebratory noise like an air horn on a DJ set.

I step forward with a hand out to introduce myself as

Anna moves forward with her arms out for a hug, causing me to almost poke her in the stomach.

"Sorry!" I say, stepping back as Anna laughs.

"It's cool, I'm a hugger – is that okay or would you prefer a handshake?" she asks, lowering her arms slightly.

Trying to recover, I shake my head quickly and move my arms out of the way, "No, no, hugs are awesome." Maybe a bit much, but it gets us across the line into a hug. Her hair is just under my face and whatever perfume or shampoo she uses briefly wafts towards me. I close my eyes for a split second to breathe it in. Let's blame my job for giving me an instinct to appreciate the smell of beautiful things, and not just me being weird here.

Realising I've been holding onto her for what is clearly a bit too long, I quickly drop my arms and step away. "I'm Ryan."

Anna laughs. God it sounds beautiful. "Yes, I've heard." She smiles, looking back at Leo, who just introduced me. Man, get it together. Why is this so stressful? Maybe because she smells amazing and looks great. Much more work mode, with a smart white t-shirt tucked into her trousers, hair up in a bun and wire glasses on. But still the same friendly relaxed smile.

I rub the back of my neck out of nervous habit and smile back, "True. It's nice to see you again."

"Again?" Leo and Dani ask in time together curiously. "You guys have met?" Leo follows up.

"Briefly," Anna jumps in, "At the restaurant on Saturday. Which now explains how we both arrived at the same time waiting for our friends who stood us up."

Leo moves back towards the kitchen, opening up the space for Anna and I to follow him through to the table.

"Unusual for strangers in London to start talking to each other, but I guess Ryan's not really a Londoner yet. We grew up in Germany together."

"Ryan doesn't feel like a very German name?" Anna asks.

"Yeah, my Dad is English so he just picked a name at random it seems." I say.

"Which is also why he got such annoyingly good grades in English at school. So, did you two just start bonding over your extremely late friends?" Leo asks, indicating that we should sit down as he moves back to the fridge and grabs a beer for Anna.

"It was more a bond over my inability to choose a wine." Anna replies, taking the beer with thanks.

"Ah well, then you were a perfect match for Ryan." Leo says, stepping back to the hob to help Dani.

Anna looks over at me, wow those eyes again, and smiles. "Absolutely. Perfect match."

Dinner was delicious. Anna is great, they were right. Really inquisitive and enthusiastic. She talks about her work like it's both the love of her life and the bane of her existence. Not sure if that's a good or a bad thing.

These three have such a great bond that they fall into a natural rhythm but without feeling like you're excluded as an outsider. I remember Leo saying something about this when he met all of Dani's friends a few years ago and now I see what he meant.

We eventually get onto wedding plans and our respective roles as the right-hand man and woman of the happy couple.

"What about an engagement party?" Anna asks excitedly.

Dani and Leo look at each other.

"We did think about it," Dani begins, "but as we want to get married early next year, we thought it might be too much to organise an engagement party as well."

Anna looks crestfallen, and then excited again.

"I'll do it?" She offers at once. Dani and Leo look entertained but somehow not that surprised.

"That's really sweet of you, but honestly, it's fine, we can focus on the wedding. There will be enough to do." Dani replies.

Anna's face is still determinedly excited.

"No work at all, we can do it in a pub in a few weeks to give people enough notice. No budget needed, no booking beyond casual table requests, and I just need a guest list," she says, like the solution was so obvious we must already all be on the same page.

Dani looks thoughtful, "I mean that does sound great, but I also know you're already a bit busy Anna?" She says, thoughtfulness turning to concern on her face.

"I'll help." I say instinctively. I will? I mean of course I will. It's for Leo. Not at all because I want to stop Anna from getting overworked, which it sounds like she already is. And maybe, I can also get to know her better beyond the two evenings I've clocked up so far.

They all turn to me.

"Are you sure?" Leo asks.

"Wow so you're ready for Anna to help but when I offer…" I joke.

"Hey, I've just never seen you organise anything!" Leo laughs back.

"I organised your birthday party before. Remember?"

"Yes, when I was 18." Leo replies.

"Okay yes, over a decade ago. But the skills are still there. I assume you want this party to be *Star Wars* themed as well?"

"I didn't even want that one to be *Star Wars* themed," Leo laughs.

"I can see it now. Anakin and Padme. Sand everywhere," Anna jumps in, putting pause to what was about to become a very childish sparring match. "Or I'm thinking maybe 'no theme'? As it's short notice in a central London pub, they may object to me filling the place up with sand?" She says starting to pile up the dirty plates.

"I suppose that makes sense." Leo nods wisely, smiling at me as he starts to clear up.

I stand up to help as well, indicating for Anna to stay seated as Leo has with Dani.

"So, do you accept my offer to help?" I ask Anna before turning away, the pasta dish carefully held.

"That would be great, thank you," Anna says looking up at me. God there she goes again with those eyes and that smile. "Shall we swap numbers so we can coordinate?"

She wants my number. That's good right? Wait, it's just for this party. I don't even know if she's single, although she hasn't mentioned a partner all evening, so I would assume she is. I need to ask Leo. Wait no, I'm trying not to date. And this is one of Leo and Dani's best friends. We should just be friends. I could do with some good friends right now. It's just a shame this particular friend makes me want to tuck her hair behind her ear and pull her face up to mine and …. no Ryan, steady on that's not friendship.

"Yeah, sounds good." I come back with, instead of proposing we just go sit together on the sofa and act out that scene playing in my mind.

Dani gets up my number to send to Anna while I turn back to the kitchen. This is your new friend Anna. Your new 'nothing romantic or intimate at all' friend Anna who you're going to plan a party with. I might need to be careful what I wish for with this friendship thing.

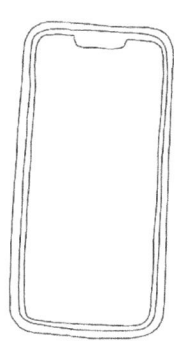

Chapter 9. Her.

Ryan. Handsome Man is Ryan. That's a hot name. If names had classifications. Anyway, it doesn't matter that he's so hot and his name's Ryan because most importantly he's now my counterpart in supporting the wedding planning. My new friend Ryan. My new incredibly handsome friend Ryan.

For a split second a thought sparks in my head, like a nervously flickering flame – what if he's single? And he likes me? And our friendly conversation is the start of something special? But a moment later I stop that train of thought in its tracks, slamming the emergency brakes on the warm feeling threatening to grow inside. I've been down this particular disaster route before. For instance, the lovely man in the sauna. Or the guy from work who flirted with me until I found him on Instagram, and discovered he's engaged. I won't list them all but consider it a lesson learned.

Take a breath. Back to reality. This is Leo's best friend, a new close friend of Dani's, and now a new friend to me too. Nothing to worry about.

I left dinner a little early as I'm pretty tired and up at 6:30am for work tomorrow as usual, so I'm now walking to the DLR by myself.

I get out my phone as I wait for the train and bring up Dani's text, clicking through to start a message to the new number. A year of rotational dating has taught me how to start texting someone on WhatsApp without having to save their number first. It's not like I'm regularly going through and reviewing my contacts, but something about giving someone a permanent place in your phone is too much when you're expecting them to be temporary. There are only a few people in the past year who have graduated to contact status, and now I don't talk to any of them anymore. Their saved numbers and names are the only evidence of the time we spent together.

As I start typing a message to Ryan his profile picture loads up, prompting me to click through on instinct. A picture of him smiling with a glass of wine in a restaurant next to a beautiful rock cove.

"Hey it's Anna! Lovely re-meeting you this eve. Let me know when works this week to do some event planning :)" I finally send, after re-typing three different versions, and then reminding myself that it doesn't matter because he's just a friend. It doesn't matter if he's the most good-looking man you've maybe ever seen, or the fact that his kind brown eyes make you want to melt into a puddle. Or preferably into his arms, which looked incredible under his light jumper this evening.

Hitting send, I throw my phone into my bag.

The engagement party plans are already fully formed in my head. Once Dani sends the guest list, I'll call a few pubs to ask for a table, set a time, make a group chat and send the invite as priority one. Then work out what fun decor or extra things we can do as priority two. Maybe some bunting or pictures on the tables? Should someone give a brief speech? Who would be the best person for this?

My train of thought is interrupted as I step back above ground at Old Street station and start walking North to my flat. After spending all of today either sitting or walking short distances between meetings, it's nice to get a bit of fresh (highly polluted) air. The sultry sounds of Zach Bryan's new album through my headphones carries me home with the right balance of calm and soothing to keep me thinking about work. A few points on my to do list can't help but pop into my head as I get into bed. But as I go to write them in my phone notes, I see a message from Ryan.

"Lovely re-meeting you too! What about Friday after work?"

Friday. Sooner rather than later would be best if we want to plan it as soon as possible. But I will also probably be in the office until 6pm earliest, then drive home. I won't be free until 7:30pm – but if that's the time that works best for him, let's make it work. In a minor act of self-preservation, I won't suggest meeting in person. We can call to organise, then I can keep working and go to bed.

"Great. I'm free to call at 7:30ish when I get home if that works?"

Ryan agrees.

Thursday passes in a blur, the highlight being a riding lesson after work with the most beautiful horse called Eddy. I like to think he has a special connection with me. He probably has that with every rider because he's a well-trained horse, but it felt special to me. This is partly because he is enormous, so it was like flying around the paddock. The sense of freedom was incredible and only slightly marred by a missed call from my manager when I got back to my car.

My favourites list on my phone includes my closest friends, my family members, and my manager – so her calls always come through, even when my phone is on Do Not Disturb. The nice thing about riding is I leave my phone in the car so it's a rare time she literally can't reach me.

I call her back on my way home, all ready for whatever next steps are coming. We're working on restructuring the team, another lovely part of managing an operational team – wait no, we can't call it a restructure because people panic. We're working on re-aligning our team roles and responsibilities.

Together with the rest of the leadership team, we had a four-hour session on Tuesday to map out the new structure. My manager was calling to check in on how it's going. I run her through the feedback on the call as I drive into London. Generally, my team has taken it well, although that's only after I spent an hour reassuring them they are valued, and not about to be made redundant.

She seems pleased and we chat through what's needed next. Nothing too complicated, it's all in my head I just need to draw up a deck of slides to put it on a screen.

It's almost dark by the time I get home, so a quick dinner and bed is waiting for me once the next steps are done.

By Friday I am in my usual, semi-dazed state of hyperactive productivity, mixed with a nice cocktail of fatigue. Realising it's almost 6:30pm, and I'm still furiously preparing my weekly governance reports at my desk, I pack up rapidly and hurry to my car to get back in time for the call with Ryan. I shoot him a quick text to say I'll be 5 mins late to stop myself speeding down the motorway.

Once home, I dump my stuff, get my headphones out and text Ryan to say I'm free when he is, seeing his sweet reply saying not to worry about being late.

Leaning against the kitchen counter for a brief second of headspace, I jump as my phone starts to ring. Video call, okay fair enough. Looking at my own slightly frazzled face I wish it was audio but here we go.

Clicking accept I see his handsome face fill the screen. "Evening." He says.

"Evening. Sorry I'm late," I say, quickly re-positioning my phone to try and optimise the angles and lighting. Then remembering he's just a friend, it doesn't matter. A very handsome friend.

"No problem, I'm in this evening anyway," he replies, "Do you mind if I cook while we chat?"

God that's hot.

"Go for it, I'm going to get my dinner ready as well." I put the phone down on the counter, propping it up against the fruit bowl while I get my food ready. "This does make me feel like an influencer though."

"You must have some very wholesome influencers on your timeline," Ryan says, carrying his phone through to the kitchen and doing the same. I can see a very nice domestic looking kitchen in the background with pictures of some girls up on the fridge. The girlfriend and friends I assume.

"Pretty wholesome. Makes me wonder what's not so wholesome on your timeline though?" I joke as I pull my next ready meal from the freezer and put it into the microwave.

Ryan seems to blush even through the phone, how adorable. "Not 'not-wholesome', just more intense maybe. I can't seem to escape being told to train for Hyrox at the moment. I don't even know what it is, but it seems like following two cross trainers on Instagram has pushed me right into it."

"If you want wholesome, Hyrox definitely isn't it. You need to start strategically liking pictures of cakes and puppies to balance it out." Ryan laughs as he moves back to open the fridge. He has such a nice laugh it makes me feel all warm inside. Time to get back on topic.

"Anyway, that could go down a total rabbit hole, although rabbits would also be good content for the feed…But back to engagement party planning, first of all, thank you so much for offering to help out."

"Of course, it sounds like you already have it planned in your head. But you shouldn't have to do it all yourself," he says, now leaning over a chopping board. Is he wearing – an apron? Oh wow. A stripy apron over a well fitted white t-shirt, I may melt. And politely offering to help me so I don't have to do it all. Goodness, nice guys in long, steady relationships really are built differently.

I jump into the proposed plans and he agrees that they all sound great. Despite my not wanting to actually ask him to do anything, he offers to sort out calling the pubs and booking the space if I let him know where I'd suggest. I send him a few spots I think would work best and agree to make the group chat and send the invite. I also run through my ideas for the decoration of the space if we have time and the pub allows it.

By this point, I'm sitting at the table eating my dinner and May is home, waving from the doorway. She looks confused as she sees my phone screen with what looks like a cooking demo video as Ryan works through stirring a large pot on the stove.

He agrees to check if we can decorate and says he'll let me know by the end of tomorrow which pub we're going for.

"Do you plan a lot of these things then?" he asks, turning back to face the camera. He now has a full view of me eating chilli, very glamorous.

"Engagement parties? Not that often, no."

"More like parties in general, it seems to be coming naturally to you."

"Sometimes things like this just make sense to me. Like, it's obvious what needs doing so I just want to do it. It's part of what keeps me so busy at work because I can't help picking up everything I can find a solution for. Parties are the best though, in another life I think I would have made a great party planner for children's birthdays."

Ryan laughs, "Specifically children's birthday parties?".

"Yeah, it seems so much more fun than for adults, and you get the best party food and can pick a fun theme. My favourite party theme is basically pop princess. Lots of pink, so much food you can barely see the table, flowers, sparkles, temporary tattoos. What would your dream parallel job be then?" I ask back. I feel like I was talking too much again.

Ryan pauses over his food, looking into the dish thoughtfully. "Not sure, I do really love working with wine and food. Maybe setting up a shop for myself."

"I think you call that a restaurant."

He laughs and looks back at the phone, leaning down on the counter to look directly at me. This new angle shows off his arms and broad shoulders even more than before, he's becoming almost distressingly sexy. "Not quite, more like a deli. Nice selection of essentials for any good kitchen, or anyone who doesn't know what the right wine is for a special occasion. Maybe throw a coffee shop on the side to keep the traffic coming. Could sell specialty coffee alongside the wine to cover more audiences and price points."

"Sounds like you've got a plan for that too then," I say. I feel like I can see the plan fully formed behind his eyes through the screen. A quiet vision.

"Does sound like it, though I didn't realise it was there until now," he says, looking thoughtful again.

I see a woman walk by in the background and grab

something out of the fridge then walk out again. Okay, that's enough bonding for one evening.

Ryan looks like he's about to say something, but before he can, I jump in, "I should probably tidy up." He closes his mouth and leans back off the counter, picking up his phone to give me a more zoomed in view of his handsome face.

"Thanks so much for helping out. I think it's going to be great," I say, smiling at the phone.

"Me too. Let me know if there's anything else you want me to help with in the meantime."

"Thanks – have a nice evening! Bye!" I call out, pressing the red end call button.

Ryan's face disappears and I'm staring back at my empty phone screen, showing his unknown number in my call logs.

I sigh as I put the phone down and start tidying up, waving to May who's sitting on the sofa taking out her headphones.

"Who was that?" she asks.

"Ryan, Leo's Best Man. Otherwise known as Handsome Saturday Night Man. He's offered to help organise their engagement party which is actually really great," I say, having already caught May up on the drama of the week and our surprise double meeting.

May gives me a secretive smile.

"What?" I ask, loading my dishes away.

"Felt like a lot of non-engagement party chat there, a bit of smiling at your phone…" she says looking excited.

"Friendly smiling, he has a girlfriend," I say, which feels sufficiently confirmed by the woman walking by in his flat.

May's face falls. I really love her investment in the potential romantic drama.

"More importantly the party is basically planned. So invites will be sent out tomorrow and then I can plan decor," I say, closing the dishwasher and walking over to sit on the sofa.

"Because productivity is always more important," May says in her knowing way.

"Exactly," I say, ignoring the pointed therapy advice in there.

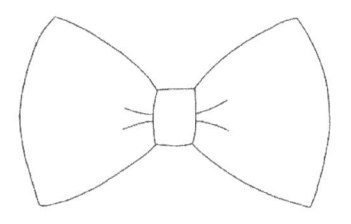

Chapter 10. Him.

I don't mean to seem paranoid. But it feels as though every time the conversation starts to get going, Anna cuts it off. This has only happened twice, so I am potentially reading too much into it. She's busy, has her own life and barely knows me. It was nice talking to her though, really easy and natural – even if it was brief.

The next day, I call the pubs and book two long tables at a place from Anna's list for the engagement party in a couple of weeks.

Texting Anna the good news, I confirm that the pub is happy with all her proposed decor suggestions (bunting, confetti on the table, balloons). She replies straight away, "Amazing thank you so much! I'll make the group and send the invite now."

True to her word, just one minute later it's done. She must have had that invite ready to go. This is next level efficiency.

It's only been a few days but it's all planned. People have started replying already with excited emojis in the chat. A slight sense of anxiety flares up at the thought of this huge social gathering, but Leo will be there. And Anna, if she talks to me for more than a moment.

Putting my phone down I lean back in my chair and look at my computer screen.

"You look like you're facing something truly existential on there," Nicki says from her place opposite me. We're sitting at our small work from home set up in our lounge. London flats on tight budgets sadly do not come with a study.

"Facing a big social event. Lots of new people," I say, moving my mouse around a pitch deck for some new suppliers while I try to work out what to start on next.

"That sounds like a good thing for someone who keeps insisting they have no friends?" Nicki says, turning back to her screen. She has a point.

"I need to turn existentialism to enthusiasm. Some of that British stiff upper lip, is that it?"

"Or just try to relax and enjoy yourself?" she suggests. Like it's so easy.

Now that Leo is back, my Saturday is lined up with activities more exciting than sitting alone reading a book or working. In preparation for their imminent nuptials, we are going suit shopping. Leo has always had bold yet excellent taste, so this is probably going to be something more inspiring than the standard dark navy suit.

He's standing outside a café in Spitalfields Market, staring up at the church at the end of the street, when I bump him on the shoulder to say hello. We're of similar height and build, a pair of 6'2" brunettes with matching sets of dark stubble. But where my features are softer, he has the chiselled bone structure of an understated indie singer. Bastard.

"Picturing the big day already?" I ask standing by his side to look up at the church.

"Hardly. We're not getting married in a church, that would be weird for two non-religious people." he says, walking into the coffee shop.

"But the buildings are so nice, maybe it's worth it just for that?" I suggest, turning to follow Leo.

If he hadn't led me into it, I would have walked right past this place. It looks like an old grocery store with wooden panelling and a faded painted front. Only when I step through the door do I notice the sleek, modern sign on the corner that reads 'Nagare Coffee'. Inside, the charm of the old shop style continues with a cosy fireplace, intimate tables, and a large wooden counter topped with an invitingly robust coffee machine. Places like this are what I adore about European cities – preserving pieces of history while crafting something refreshingly new.

Leo picks out a coffee for me, which we drink as we walk towards the suit shop he wanted to visit.

"Do you know what you're looking for?" I ask as we walk down a narrow street past the church.

"Well, as it's for Spring, something light but warm enough. Maybe something colourful."

"Practical and stylish as always."

The shop we've arrived at houses a collection of colourful materials and well-made suits. I start browsing on instinct as Leo looks around.

"Your engagement party is coming along nicely. Anna's done a great job pulling it together so quickly. She's already bought all the decor. Sorry – surprise decor, pretend you didn't hear that," I say, my mind going to the wedding and guests, or (if I'm honest) to one guest in particular.

"She's like Dani, super organised especially for stuff like this. You should have seen the way they booked our California trip last year with Sam, another of their friends from home. Smashed it out in a few hours and had the Splitwise settled by the end of the day," Leo says fondly, picking up a light green suit and holding it up in the mirror.

"Impressive effort," I say, thinking of Anna and how excited she looked while party planning. She must reach a whole other level for something bigger like a holiday. I wonder what sort of things she likes to do on holiday. I know they were hiking – is that her standard activity plan? Does she go hiking around London?

Leo clears his throat to bring my attention back to him as he holds up the suit with a questioning face.

"Sorry – very dashing," I say, bringing my focus back to the suits as Leo steps into the changing rooms.

I saw the pictures of their California trip but remember mainly mountains, not people. I didn't realise that Anna was there too. This was during the depths of Karina's and my extended low point as a couple. I wasn't very observant of anything except trying to find a job so we could make our next move together. Clearly not time well spent.

"Do you know where you guys are getting married yet?" I ask through the curtain.

"I think we're going to choose one of the Cambridge Uni venues. Dani grew up in Cambridge and her family lives there, so it makes sense – plus the halls are really nice."

I make a sceptical noise as I pick up a set of tartan bow ties. "I mean, sure, if you want to be predictable, go for something historic and classic. Why not go back to your German roots and get married in a castle? Or a beer hall?" I suggest in my most fake serious tone.

"Great shout. We can bring our cultures together and get married in a Wetherspoons so Dani feels at home," Leo says without a beat from behind the dressing room curtain.

"Exactly. Provide nothing but scones and currywurst," I say, holding up a purple velvet suit which makes me feel like Willy Wonka. "See, I'm such a good Best Man. So many good suggestions. You're welcome."

Leo steps out of the changing room in the suit and looks at me.

"Just as I start coming up with these great ideas you show me up with even better ones. I would have said light green wouldn't work, but you've stepped out like some kind of German-forest-prince-James Bond to prove me wrong," I say with an overdramatic sigh, putting the velvet back on the rack.

Leo grins at me, looking in the mirror, "I like it too."

That man rightfully has the self-confidence of a King.

"Is this about to be the easiest shopping experience ever? I was expecting a long line of outfits, throwing cufflinks across the room, some tears?"

"Maybe we'll save that for the wedding." Leo says, stepping onto the platform so the tailor can start taking his measurements.

"Are you expecting any more substantial wedding drama?" I ask, leaning against the shelves of ties behind me.

"Not really. My family is pretty relaxed as you know, and Dani's family is small but all really friendly. Dani moved over from Korea with her mum when she was young, so they are really close," Leo says.

"Damn I can't imagine how hard that must have been. Moving from Germany as an adult who speaks perfect English is hard enough settling in. Not saying Dani's Mum couldn't speak English, I didn't mean-" I reply, conscious of the assumptions I'm making mid-sentence.

Leo smiles at me calmly, "Don't worry mate. You're not wrong, I think it was tough. As it's just her and her mum, I think Dani is keen to move closer to her when we move out of London."

"It must mean a lot, you're joining their family," I say, thinking about how it must feel becoming part of such a tight knit group.

My family is a bit more sprawling. My older brother and sister are both living in Germany with their long-term partners. We're not super close, all having gone our separate ways as adults, but it always fits back into the normal familiar rhythm when we get back together. My parents still live out in the countryside, next to Leo's parents, where we grew up.

They host us all for a few weeks each Summer, and each of us makes the effort to join in. It's the time we all get to recharge and reconnect as a family, and it's a highlight for me every year.

Leo's family is like Dani's. He's an only child so it's just him and his parents. Which is probably why he spent so much time messing around at my house with me and my siblings instead.

Leo isn't having any other groomsmen apart from me, so I choose a similar but darker green suit so that we're matching but not identical. It's taking me a little out of my comfort zone to be wearing something a bit more colourful. I normally stick to a standard uniform of blue, black, and white to blend in. As it's a darker green it's not too bold, and it's nice to match with Leo. On the subject of family, he's definitely part of mine. I'll happily wear something a little different for his special day.

I wonder what Anna will be wearing.

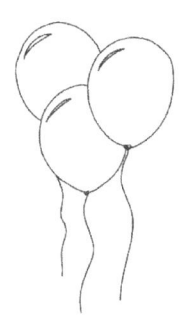

Chapter 11. Her.

Everything was supposed to be done two hours ago. But I am somehow still on my laptop shuffling data around an excel to get something urgent finished. How do these requests not get cascaded down until three hours before? Did no one really know the CEO wanted it for today for the event this weekend? Regardless, the result is the same: I am not going to be able to pick up the decorations for the party before the shop closes. I may not even be at the party on time at this rate. I was meant to be finishing a little early to set everything up (not sure how I thought that would be the case). Now it's an hour before people are due to arrive and there's no way I'm getting out any time soon.

Okay deep breaths. It's okay if I'm not the first to arrive. The decorations are also not essential for the party. If I don't get them, it won't ruin everything. No one even knows that there are meant to be decorations. It doesn't matter. I say this to myself but still feel an intense sense of failure – like the party is ruined. I'm letting down Dani and Leo by not doing a good enough job to create something special for them.

I move away from my laptop and lean back in my chair. I'm in the Farringdon office today because it should theoretically be easier to get to the party store and then to the pub from here. Normally, this office is great – really buzzy, with the tech teams bringing a fantastic energy. The lower-level windows are eclipsed by other buildings, but the top floor has a stunning view across the city. Arriving in the morning to see a pink sky behind St. Paul's is always worth the early start in my book.

However, at the end of the day on Friday, the office is deserted. The lights keep going off, and I find myself wheeling my chair back and forth to trigger them back on – a humbling reminder that it's time to leave.

I pick up my phone for a momentary distraction, hoping to calm myself down and help me think straight.

A few unread messages pop up, including one from an unsaved number. Someone from the Feeld roster? Wait no, I put those into archive. Hey Harper telling me about the latest sale maybe?

"Hey, let me know if you need any help with setting up today." Opening it up, I realise it's Ryan.

What was it he said? I shouldn't have to do it all myself. Does he actually mean it?

Well, at this point it's a Hail Mary because I won't be able to get it all done anyway, so no harm in asking.

"Actually, I've gotten caught up at work so I won't be able

to pick up the decorations. No worries if not, but any chance you could pick them up on the way? Don't worry about the balloons and stuff, but there's a 'congratulations' banner that would be nice to hang. No problem if not! I should hopefully be there just before it starts." I re-read it. Do I need another 'no worries!' – I don't have the time or headspace for this. I send it and forward a screenshot of the confirmation email with all the details.

I know Sam, another Sixth Form bestie, will be there early. I shoot him a text letting him know I may be late and ask if he can grab the tables and settle in before people arrive. Okay, it's covered. Everything will be fine. People will show up and celebrate. I can finish my reporting summary now.

7pm comes and goes and I am finally shutting down my laptop and running to the lift. I am going to be late to the event I helped organise, man I am a terrible friend. I don't check my phone because I can't face the stress and head straight to the bus to go to the George & Vulture in Hoxton. Not so obvious a choice for Dani and Leo who live Southeast, but they wanted somewhere central to make it easier for everyone else.

It's a great classic London pub, high ceilings, wooden floors, tables, and bar. The lines of drinks behind the bar give a soft warm glow over the room, matched on the other side with the fairy lights adorning the windows. Ideal for hosting as the staff are fantastic and the drinks are always well poured. None of this 'two inches of head per pint' nonsense.

Pausing outside, I stop for a breath again. It's going to be fine. I'm only thirty minutes late, they may not even be here yet.

I walk in with a façade of calm and am met with an explosion of decorations. The room is overflowing with hordes of balloons, banners and bunting. 'Congratulations Dani & Leo' hangs elegantly across the back wall over the mismatch of artwork.

It's just how I pictured it. Actually, it's better, because I would never would have asked to decorate quite so excessively.

Spotting Sam and his girlfriend, Stella, standing nearby, I weave through the crowd to greet them with hugs and hellos. Despite the stress of the moment, I can't help but admire their coordinated outfits. Sam's white knit jumper and navy trousers perfectly complement Stella's navy silk dress and knit cardigan, her long red hair cascading in flawless waves down her back. Sam has always had good taste, but Stella's elegance has clearly inspired him to elevate his style. She effortlessly pulls off a pearl necklace and silk dress in a pub, making her look chic yet relaxed.

"This looks amazing, thank you so much! I know I said to settle in early, but how did you manage this?"

Sam looks surprised, "I didn't do any of this, we only just arrived as our bus was delayed – Leo's friend said this was all you?" Sam gestures with a chunky knit covered arm across the room to where a set of broad shoulders in a light blue shirt is standing against the bar looking at the beer selection.

"You did a fantastic job though it's so festive! Dani and Leo are going to love it." Stella adds while I keep looking across in amazement. The party is set up and looks great, better, than planned. The room is already rammed with Dani and Leo's other friends from home, university, and work. It's a beautiful testimony to how beloved they are, seeing the room full of happy chatter like this. The nervous pressure pushing against my chest starts to soften.

I say thanks to Sam and Stella then quickly open my bag. I really want to say thank you to Ryan, but I have an important admin task to tick off first. Pulling out a book and putting it on the table, I lean back to grab Sam and Stella.

"Can you guys sign this and get other people to as well?" I ask, handing them a pen each.

"Stop Anna, this is so nice…" Sam says, looking down at the next piece of the party.

I had a brain wave last night when I was too wired to sleep. To try and stop myself from spiralling on work or anything personal, I focused on potential ways to make the party more special – based on what craft supplies I could source in less than 24 hours.

I decided to recreate something I had at my Batmitzvah. It's a book of printed pictures of Dani and Leo, with spaces on each page for signatures and cute messages.

After doing an intense photo haul on my phone at 2am, delving into long forgotten Instagram posts, I printed and stuck the pictures into a book early this morning in the office before work. Obviously I had a stack of cute notepads ready to go, and between May and I we had a few sparkly sharpies on hand, so it was an easy gift.

Leaving Stella and Sam to write, I start heading to the bar, but as I walk over a loud cheer erupts as Dani and Leo walk in. Even the bartenders start cheering. The team spirit in here is just delightful.

Dani beelines towards me, "Anna this is too much! Thank you!"

"Honestly I barely did anything," I say, looking back at Ryan who had been similarly accosted by Leo.

"Sure, sure," Dani says smiling, leading me towards the bar. "I think a celebratory drink is in order."

"I second that," Ryan calls from the other side of Leo.

Looking up at him I feel so incredibly grateful for all he's done here. I can barely get the words out and thankfully Dani passes me a pint of something so I don't have to right now.

"To you guys," I say, raising my glass for a toast. Dani and Leo smile as we clink our glasses together. Just as I take a sip, I look at Ryan and we hold eye contact for a moment too long, feeling a bit too familiar.

Once Dani and Leo move away to greet their guests, I step towards Ryan. "Thank you so much for doing this," I begin, struggling to convey how much it means to me. It might seem trivial but relying on someone else is a big ask for me. When they not only come through, but also make a real effort, it means a lot.

"You must love Leo a lot to go through all this effort."

Ryan pauses for a second, tilting his head like he's considering his answer.

"Well of course, he's my best friend you know." We turn to watch them move through the crowd of well-wishers.

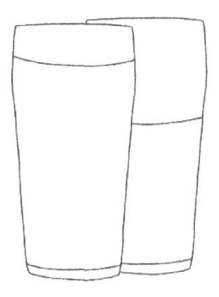

Chapter 12. Him.

It's that smell of flowers and apricots. Is it perfume, shower gel, or is it something else I don't know? It reminds me of the fields of wildflowers behind my parents' house in summer, of lying in the sun and feeling at home. Of something warm and comforting. And it's very distracting as I stand here. It's also distracting that Anna's wearing a very tight t-shirt over a long dark skirt and white boots. They make her legs look even longer.

I'm trying not to get too distracted picturing her thighs wrapped around me because I'm not going to act on it. But for some reason, all I can think about right now is kneeling next to her and slowly sliding my hands up under her skirt as I kiss her stomach. It's just an idea…that for some reason I can't get out of my head.

I just need to ignore it. I'm still in 'relationship recovery mode', as I'm now calling it to myself. I've set the mental timeline of getting my life set up properly in London first and giving my breakup some distance. A relationship can come second.

In the interim, helping Anna has been nice. It was easy really. She had already spoken so excitedly about how she envisioned the pub set up. When she said she couldn't make it to pick up the decorations, it was like an open invite to turn her dream into a reality. The biggest challenge was flailing around with the bunting (because who knew how that was supposed to work?), but the bar staff took pity on me and helped deck the place out pretty quickly.

If she wants to say it's just because of my friendship with Leo, that's probably easier. It's probably coming on a bit strong to say otherwise, so this helps keep my potential friendship with Anna on track. In reality, I just wanted to do something nice for her. Sure, the décor is festive and makes it more party-like, but the party would be essentially the same without it. Anna seemed so excited about doing this extra thing for her friends. I knew how disappointed she would be if it didn't turn out as she had hoped, and it felt good making her life a little easier.

It turns out it wasn't even that big of a help because she also seems to have organised a personalised guest book as well. I feel a strange pang wondering why she didn't mention it or ask me to help.

Before I can find the right way to bring it up, two people come over. I met them briefly on arrival but didn't catch their names.

"Sam, Stella – have you met Ryan?" Anna says, getting

everyone up to speed.

"Hey man, we saw you earlier but didn't get a chance to say hi properly. I'm Sam, this is Stella," Sam says, indicating a glamorous woman standing next to him with an arm around his waist.

"Hey," she says, smiling at me.

Sam has dark curly hair in a mullet, so I'm surprised when he says he works as a consultant at some big firm. Anna adds how busy and hardcore he is as work, looking very proud and clearly refusing to let Sam undersell himself.

The conversation flows easily as everyone catches up on their days and weeks. Stella is training to be an accountant so replays her latest exams which sound impossibly difficult.

"Sounds like you need a good break once those are done," I say, happy everything is going smoothly with the party and some new potential friends. I'm also trying to drag my eyes away from looking at Anna standing next to me. Our shoulders are touching ever so slightly, but I don't move away and neither does she. It feels strangely comforting having her by my side.

"I wish. But I have more exams in January, so there's maybe one weekend where I could have a proper break before starting to study again," Stella says sadly. Sam gives her a kiss on the forehead as a gentle piece of support.

"Well then, that's the perfect weekend for a break," Anna replies, looking as excited and inspired as she did when suggesting the engagement party.

"How about a weekend in Cambridge? If you're up for a break away from home?"

Stella and Sam look at each other, doing some quick silent relationship communications in a single glance.

"That would be great actually. If I'm in London I'll probably just start studying again, so a weekend away may be the perfect distraction," Stella says, turning back to the group with a smile.

"Great! We just need to rope in the happy couple," Anna says looking over at Dani and Leo. "I can check if my parents are happy for us to use their house for the weekend and we're good to go."

I'm just wondering if I should try and slide away to let them finish planning when Anna turns to me expectantly.

"You and your girlfriend are obviously invited as well – us Wedding Party Generals have to stick together," she says, holding her hand up in a salute.

Two shocks in one. Firstly, that I'm invited. Our conversations have been great so far but I wasn't getting the impression that Anna was very interested in spending time with me. I must have underestimated her friendliness. Secondly, girlfriend?

"Are you sure?" I ask, also very conscious this may be an invite out of pity as I'm standing here while they plan. "I don't want to impose, it feels like a lot of people."

"Not at all!" Anna says in a welcoming manner that makes it clear she wouldn't want it any other way. "My parents have space for three couples plus me so it's an easy fix up. We would love to have you join the gang."

Looking across at Sam and Stella they look genuinely keen as well. Here goes, more socialising.

"Okay well then that would be great, as long as you're sure it's not an inconvenience," Anna shakes her head with a smile. "But it'll just be me coming."

Her smile turns to a frown, "Honestly, it's not a fuss to have an extra person, please feel free to bring your plus one. It's not a closed invite."

"I appreciate that, but I don't have anyone else to invite apart from Leo," I say, not sure how else to say that without making it sound sad.

Anna seems to frown even more for a split second but regains herself quickly, "Oh sorry my bad, I thought the woman you lived with-"

"That's my flatmate, Nicki. I mean, I do like her, but just as a friend. Which I'm sure her boyfriend is happy about as well," I joke. I'm not quite sure why this is an important detail, but I feel like I have to justify being friends with my female flatmate in the face of this strange assumption.

"Cool okay, makes mealtimes an easier fix for 6 not 7," Anna says. Her face looks a little flushed all of a sudden, maybe it's just the warmth of the room.

Her and Sam immediately start planning potential activities. They both grew up in Cambridge with Dani so they are debating which touristy things would land best with the newbies and what's feasible in the middle of November, when it's likely to be raining ("You can't punt with umbrellas!" "Not with that attitude!").

As the party is in full swing, Anna excuses herself to call the group to attention.

"Hey everyone! Thanks so much for coming! I know a lot

of people came from out of town, so I appreciate all the effort. To celebrate the occasion, Clare is going to say a few words about the happy couple!" She shouts cheerfully, bringing not only the party, but the whole pub to turn and look. I'm blown away by the amount of effort she's put into something that was meant to be 'no work'. The complete lack of self-consciousness and courage to jump into something with all these different people amazes me.

One of Dani's University friends steps forward and starts giving a very sweet and funny speech. It's only as the speech is wrapping up, after a lot of laughter, that I notice Anna back at my side drinking her pint in a celebratory toast with everyone else.

"Great choice of speaker," I say, impressed. "I also saw the guest book, it's really thoughtful."

"Thanks," she says with a happy smile, which drops suddenly as she turns to put her drink on the bar and look at me. Her hands seem to be tensely wrapped around each other, like she's trying to build up the courage to say something uncomfortable. I brace myself to be uninvited from the weekend away.

"And thank you for helping get everything together for this. I really, really appreciate it," she says, moving for a second like she's about to touch my arm. Instead, she puts her hands back down, tangled together again.

I let out a breath as I hold her gaze. She looks so earnestly grateful for something that feels so small that I'm not sure what to say apart from, "You're welcome."

Chapter 13. Her.

I'm not sure if organising social events can be called an addiction, but if it is, I have it. I'm not sorry I love organised fun.

It also provides a great distraction from work, because nothing distracts me from work like another kind of work. If you completely jam your schedule with activities, there's no time to think about all the things that make you feel like you're going to explode. That's how you solve problems, right? Hide from them and hope they disappear?

I have previously used dates and sex for escapism. 'Previous' being a generous term for 'up until 2 weeks ago'. But I'm trying to reign that back. Hence putting the dating app roster in archive and trying to ride more after work instead. Horses that is.

It's only been a couple of weeks of this new approach, but I think it's having a good impact. I'm still biting my nails so aggressively on the drive home that it's become painful to take out my retainer, but at least I'm getting an occasional early night and a bit more sleep. I've replaced my after-work routine from drinks-sex-shower-bed to dinner-shower-bed. Less alcohol and sleep deprivation, more vegetables. I'm no scientist, but surely that's a recipe for success?

Organising the weekend in Cambridge is simple. We agreed on a weekend in late November once Stella's exams are done. I'm going to drive up a few days before to stay with my parents before they go away, as it lines up with a weekend when they are visiting friends in Devon. So the house will be empty for a hoard of millennials to descend. And by descend, I mean have dinner with drinks and watch movies.

In the meantime, I've been keeping busy with socialising, exercise, and lots of work. I haven't spoken to Ryan since the engagement party and learning of his single status. Knowing he's single makes it harder for me to put him in the 'you will not date them' box. Not impossible, but harder. He fitted in that box perfectly before. I could appreciate how beautiful he is with only a slight sense of wishful longing.

Now, knowing there's a glimmer of potential complicates things. I have to be stricter in my mind to set the boundary that it won't happen. It's the hope that kills you and the idea of considering that something romantic might happen is too frightening. I've been hurt too many times in the past year, I can't face putting myself out there again.

I'm recounting a lighter version of these events to May on our walk around South Kensington. We're doing one of our regular flatmate date days to get in some quality time –

because living together isn't enough.

Today's agenda is the Victoria & Albert Museum (my favourite museum in London), coffee breaks, and a stop in the wine shop to pick up something for dinner this evening.

"If you're nervously avoiding this guy, why are we going to his place of work?" May asks, taking a sip of her pumpkin spice chai latte as we walk.

It's now mid-October and London is in full autumn mode. Gorgeous leaves, themed snacks, plus the perfect weather for light layers, means it is easily the best season. It's especially perfect in London where the parks begin to glow with golds and browns, and everywhere you look the locals are wrapped up with warm drinks and knitwear.

I roll my eyes. "I'm not avoiding him. I love chatting to him and he has a face that looks like it was carved by angels. But we're not like, friends? So why would I text him to hang out? And I'll see him in a few weeks so it's hardly avoiding. He's literally going to be at my house."

May looks unimpressed, as she is a strong endorser of facing emotions instead of hiding from them. But just because this man is single doesn't mean he would want to date me at all. He's still in the 'you will not date them' box. Nothing has changed.

"And we're not going to his place of work," I continue. "He's a buyer, he doesn't work in the shop. Anyway, it's desperate times. I can't serve my parents subpar wine with dinner, it's just embarrassing," I add, concluding with what feels like a very reasonable argument.

"Yes, you're right, they will probably just disown you if

you serve them bad wine," May says seriously.

"Exactly. Familial bonds over. Rejection. Disgrace."

Checking my phone again to find the right spot, I lead us through more winding, picturesque rows of clean white terrace houses until we find the shop. The classy front awning and lines of neatly laid bottles tells me we are in the right place.

As we walk in, the gentle smell of wood and wine hangs in the air, like the soothing back porch on a ranch. There's a couple of men standing with their backs to us looking at something on the desk.

"We'll be with you in one minute!" One of them turns to say. He's a middled aged man with a pair of dark glasses and an unexpectedly jazzy tie for such a demure shop. He turns back to his colleague, a younger blonde man with his back still to us.

"No rush," I say calmly as we turn to start browsing the white wine collection. It's allegedly a good pairing for the fish I'm cooking this evening.

May and I start picking out our favourite wine labels quietly, discussing whether you should judge a wine by its label, like a book by its cover. I'm about to ask May what she would call her wine label and what the logo would be when a hand taps me on the shoulder with a "Fancy seeing you here?"

Turning in surprise, I see a man that I dated for precisely seven hours at the start of this year standing holding an inventory clipboard. I honestly couldn't tell you his name if you paid me. Matt? This is the guy who did a lot of rock climbing and had a great six pack, but also had no interest in what I had to say. We spent at least two hours without him asking me a single question. He was also the one who ordered my drink before I arrived without asking what I wanted. Hence my complete lack of interest and no desire to see him afterwards. Those factors didn't stop me inviting him back to mine after a few glasses of wine for an acceptably fun time together. I had no idea he worked here. Oh god, is this how my haunted house of exes begins. Please don't let more of them be queued up outside.

"Hiiiii…." I say, lingering on the letters to hide my inability to remember his name. I go in for a hug on default, maybe a weird thing to do considering. Although we have slept together, so arguably this is far less intimate.

"Tom," he says, finishing my sentence for me with a smile of amusement. Wow I wasn't even close.

"Yes of course – Tom. Totally…this is my flatmate, May." May smiles politely, probably having already guessed how we know each other. We have a good routine of ensuring she avoids all the people I date unless they are worth saving as a contact. Tom didn't make the cut.

"Picking up something for a date?" he asks with a laugh. He's right, powering through is probably for the best so let's pretend this ended amicably. Which it sort-of did. He had texted asking if we could go out again. I said thanks but 'it was really great meeting you and I had a super fun time, but I don't think the connection is quite right'. My default let down phrase.

"Even better, dinner with my parents. We're having cod,

so something white?" I say, playing along. One bottle of wine and I'm out.

"Something good enough to balance out your cooking," May adds with an entertained smile, helping keep the friendly energy afloat.

Tom (as is apparently his name) steers us to a section of white wine and picks up a couple of bottles. "Both of these go well with most fish, but this one," he says moving one slightly towards us, "is an exclusive Chardonnay from Australia. An enjoyable and unpretentious refreshment if you're not sure what you're looking for. And its carbon neutral, they have solar panels at the vineyard to fuel production." This is already a better conversation than the three hours of our date before sex. If I get a nice bottle of wine out of it, we may beat the sex entirely.

"I'm sold," I say, and he puts the other bottle back and leads us to the counter to pay.

"What are you up to this weekend after dinner, do you want to maybe get a drink?" he asks as he scans the wine through.

"Er I…"

"Anna?" Looking back up from my hands, where I had been trying to find a good reply, I see Ryan staring back at me. He's standing in the doorway to the backroom, looking incredible in some dark jeans and a crisp white shirt which contrasts nicely with his dark hair. He's holding a wooden box in his gorgeous, strong hands.

It really is like a haunted house. The scope for the nightmare has apparently expanded beyond my exes, to my crushes too.

"Ryan hi. I didn't realise you worked here."

Ryan frowns, as I realise what I've said. "I mean, I knew you worked here," I say, gesturing at the shop as a whole. "But I didn't realise you worked…here," I finish by pointing at the floor. Smooth.

"So did you guys date too then?" Tom asks in a light hearted manner, pointing between us. This fucking guy.

"No, no, we're just friends," I say, looking at Ryan who raises his eyebrows in surprise. Either by the notion we could be dating or the notion we're friends. Not sure which is worse at this moment.

"Oh cool," Tom says looking completely nonplussed. His ability to not care is maybe more impressive than his ability to pick a wine pairing for cod. Or talk about himself for two hours straight.

"Hi! I'm May," May adds to break the ice. Ryan leans a hand forward for her to shake, "Heard all about you – loved your party contribution. Sounds like you nailed that."

Ryan blushes ever so slightly and smiles.

"Thanks, honestly I was just a helping hand. Anna sorted it all out."

"Big understatement," I say. But before I can follow up, Tom, who is clearly starting to feel left out, interrupts.

"So are you wanting to pay or what?"

I pay and we leave with a quick 'bye!', which is thankfully the most seamless parts of my time in this shop, if you ignore the painfully awkward tension remaining in the room.

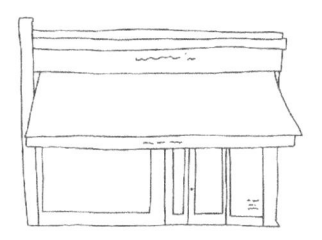

Chapter 14. Him.

Watching Anna run away is maybe the next step up from her cutting off a conversation. I wouldn't have guessed Tom would be the sort of guy she would date. To be honest, given the way they interacted, perhaps she thinks the same.

"That's a funny coincidence," Tom says, sitting in the chair behind the counter as Anna and May close the door.

"Yeah hilarious," I reply, feeling annoyed but not quite sure why. Stupid overconfident Tom with his bad customer service manner. I want to ask about their dates, but it feels strangely personal to Anna, given we're apparently friends now.

"She's wild isn't she," Tom says, seemingly to himself. Not the word I would use to describe her given our interactions so far. Kind, welcoming, and passionate maybe – even if it's just about party planning. I make a noncommittal noise, slightly nervous to keep the conversation going.

"I guess you know what they say, some women just don't know what they want," Tom continues.

"How do you mean?" Damn it, he's reeled me in.

"So, we went on a date at the start of the year. Total gentleman, buy her a glass of wine, nice evening at the Lighterman. Few rounds down, we're having a great conversation – I'm thinking, we're onto it now. Then boom, she invites me back to hers – pretty forward right? But I think – sure the chemistry is there, so let's go. We have a great time, very cosy, very couple-y, then the next day she says she doesn't want to see me again. Think she was just interested in the casual thing, didn't want a relationship or anything serious. Just smash and dash."

It all felt sufficiently reasonable until the 'smash and dash' comment.

"I don't think I can do casual," I say, still staring at the spot by the window where Anna just disappeared out of sight. Tom's complete lack of self-awareness somehow seems to be getting me to share more.

"I mean it sucks when you're not expecting it – but if you're both on board it can be great. You just need the right person," he replies. "You have to like them enough to sleep with them, but be clear you're not getting into a relationship. It's a fine line but a magical thing if you find it. Like all the benefits of a relationship with none of the emotional baggage."

I personally don't think of the emotional side of a relationship as 'baggage' but I do sort of see Tom's point. A relationship-lite. If I'm not quite ready for one. Am I ready for one? How are you supposed to know these things? My mind wanders to an image of me and Anna buying wine on a Saturday, picking out something for our dinner plans while she takes me through her latest work drama. Or I pick it up for her and make us dinner while she finds a way to relax. It could be nice.

But what if she doesn't want that? She's been keeping the friendship at arm's length, but from what Tom says maybe that's what you're supposed to do to keep it casual? Like a halfway house. If it is like a 'relationship-lite' it could be a way to spend more time together, which I feel strangely drawn to do. Or it could be a recipe for disaster; this is my best friend's - fiancée's - best friend after all.

"Pardon?" I say, as I realise Tom has been speaking for the few minutes I was thinking.

"You haven't tapped that?" he asks. Charming.

Feeling increasingly resentful at Tom and his stupid face, I grab my coat to step out for my lunch break.

"No," I say firmly as I walk out and slam the door behind me.

"I thought pilates was meant to be relaxing?" I wheeze.

"I thought you were meant to be in good shape?" Nicki laughs at me.

I look up at her from where I'm bent over with my hands on my thighs in pain. We're standing on Clapham High Street, having just done what I would refer to as 'modern torture at 9am on a Sunday morning', but is also apparently known as 'Reformer pilates'.

Unable to come up with a good come-back over the screaming pain from my muscles, I resign myself to try to stand back up slowly.

"Do you need me to carry you to Gail's?" Nicki asks. A bold offer coming from someone half my size. Although given how she completely nailed that class, while I became a shaky mess, maybe I'm underestimating her.

"No, no – I'm fine. Walk on," I say, gesturing ahead with my arm and trying to stop the pain coming through in my voice.

Nicki grabs my arm to drag me forwards, still shaking her head with laughter. We start heading towards her favourite coffee spot, just south of our flat. She's in London for a change, after many weekends away, so she kindly invited me to join her in a gym class this morning. Well, I thought it was kind, but maybe this was her way to tell me she hates me.

"Is it nice to be back in London after so many weekends away?" I ask, curious. "I'm surprised you still remember your way around."

"I could never forget the way to coffee, it's like a calling from the mothership," Nicki replies, her tone mock-serious. "But it is lovely to be back. I adore spending time with Alex's family, but I've missed my gym-coffee routine. Village life just isn't the same."

"Doesn't this count as village life?" I gesture to the neighbourhood ahead of us. It looks like a scene plucked straight from an English postcard, with charming shops, a fishmonger, a butcher, and a pet shop all nestled in between Clapham South's streets. And of course, three pubs. The pub-to-housing ratio here could be a subject of academic study.

"I know, right? It's so quaint! Just one of those little pockets of village life scattered throughout London," Nicki beams as she leads me toward the café queue.

"Would Alex ever consider moving here?" I ask, glancing around at the couples and young families enjoying their Saturday morning.

"No, I think we're planning to move to Cheshire when we move in together next year," she says, bending down to admire the enticing display of baked goods as we inch closer to the counter.

I'm still getting to know Nicki, but this surprises me. She has the most vibrant social life I've ever seen, often out with friends or hitting the gym every evening. The idea of her embracing a quieter, countryside lifestyle feels like a drastic shift.

One of the baristas approaches to take our order, and Nicki confidently leads the way, showcasing her bakery expertise. After ordering an array of treats I don't recognise, we step outside to find a table, relishing the cool air that contrasts with the warmth from our class. The outdoor setting also provides a perfect viewing platform for the parade of small dogs passing by.

"How will you survive in Cheshire without pastries like these?" I joke, lifting one of our breakfast goods.

"Don't get me started, it's going to be a killer!" Nicki exclaims, tearing into her bun. "But being closer to Alex's family will be great. We'll be able to hike and spend more time together, which is what really matters."

"That sounds lovely," I say. "It must be tough being apart so much. I also didn't realise you were such a big hiker."

Nicki makes a face as she chews. "Big is probably an overstatement, but I enjoy a nice hike, preferably one that leads to a good Aperol spritz or iced latte."

Something about her response feels off. It sounds more like Alex's reasons for moving than her own. I can't tell if she's avoiding the truth, as I did with Karina, or if she's genuinely convinced that Alex's priorities are hers as well. So far, the only reason she's given for moving is to spend more time with him. As her flatmate and a relatively new friend, I feel hesitant to pry, but I can't shake the concern.

"Finding a place to move in together can be challenging. There's so much compromise involved, it's rare to find somewhere that truly works for both people," I say, trying to frame it objectively as a shared experience. "That was the crunch point with my ex. We talked about moving in together, but she didn't consider what it would mean. When she finally expressed her doubts, it was too late, I wished she'd been more upfront earlier. Her hesitation was a sign, you know? It's great that you and Alex are having these conversations now."

Nicki nods slowly, looking thoughtfully at a young parent across the street helping their son with his bike helmet. I might be being too obvious, but hopefully the message is getting across. Food for thought.

"What about you?" Nicki says, looking back at me. "We're in the depths of cuffing season. Are you dating anyone? I don't feel like you've ever mentioned it."

I can feel my cheeks turning slightly pink in the cold, a humbling habit.

"I don't want to know what 'cuffing season' is, but I also don't think I'm quite there yet to be honest. I need to settle in a bit more. Stand on my own feet instead of just jumping into a relationship you know?"

Nicki looks surprised and impressed.

"Wow – you're beating like every other 30 something man I've ever met. Normally I'm trying to convince my male friends to wait a week before they start dating again, let alone actually reflecting on their lives at all."

"Feels like a low bar?"

"And yet – so many men just limbo under it," she says, making me laugh.

"I'm too tall to limbo."

"That must be it." Nicki pauses with the rest of her bun in her hand. "What about that girl from the party planning? Aren't you going to see her next week?"

The colour on my cheeks darkens. I'm being betrayed by my face.

"Anna? She's cool, but I think we're just friends. Or, I hope we're friends. Like I said, I'm not looking to date. And I don't think she's looking to date either," I say, very aware of the fact I'm rambling. I blame it on the coffee.

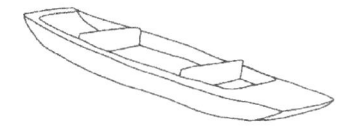

Chapter 15. Her.

Going back home to Cambridge is always like taking a breath of fresh air. The air is actually cleaner being away from London, but there's something comforting about the open space, parks, childhood memories, and knowing that my parents are there to support me if I need them. I'm incredibly lucky that way and I really appreciate it. I go back to see my parents as much as I can. It's especially valuable when work gets so crazy to have this safe, calm space to go back to. It sucks when I have to cancel social plans to go home and hibernate, but at least I have a comfortable space to hibernate in.

The sound of gravel on the driveway on Saturday morning tells me that Dani is pulling in, a full car of friends in tow. Opening the front door, I hear a wave of excited chatter as everyone gets out of the car and grabs their bags.

Leo is unloading the boot with Stella, while Sam and Dani wrestle over who gets to take out their coat first. Ryan is standing quietly at the side looking at me. He looks gorgeous as usual, in some light blue jeans and a navy Patagonia fleece. It's criminal for him to stand and look at me in such a normal way after our last ghastly interaction at the wine shop. It's also taking a lot of energy to stand and smile instead of walking over and pulling him up against me, putting my hands in his hair, bringing our faces closer together and…

"We're here!" Dani calls, throwing her arms out in celebration, coat held victoriously in hand while Sam picks his up off the floor, jolting me out of my fantasy.

"Huzzah!" I say with a flourish, stepping back as they start filtering inside in a line of hugs and hellos.

Ryan is the last to step through the doorway, "Thank you so much for inviting me along this weekend," he says, his deep brown eyes locking onto mine.

I blink up at him, feeling momentarily lost in their warmth. "No problem, it's my pleasure," I reply, trying to sound relaxed. I move in for a hug, and to my relief, he seems prepared this time, his arms moving around my waist. My instinct to hug him over the shoulders puts me in an intimate space, with my face in his neck and his arms completely wrapped around me. Without warning, he pulls me in a fraction tighter. My breath catches, and I lean into him even more, a thrill running down my spine.

Being so close, wrapped in his arms, feels electric and yet incredibly comforting – like a warm summer breeze brushing against my skin on a cold day.

As if suddenly aware of the intimacy of the moment, he begins to release me, but I can't help but keep my feet planted and lean back slightly where I stand. My fingers graze the back of his neck, touching his unbelievably soft hair as my arms slide down to linger on his shoulders. His hands rest on my hips, his thumbs making slow, gentle movements against my side. I look up, our eyes locking, and my heart seems to stop.

The warmth still radiates from where our bodies touched, but now the electricity between us crackles with intensity under my skin. It's as if the tiny specks of golden light reflecting in his eyes have ignited a cascade of sparks, flowing over me, igniting every nerve ending.

Time stretches into a heartbeat, or maybe several hours – I can't tell. Suddenly, a loud clang in the kitchen breaks the spell, causing me to jump back and exhale a breath I hadn't realized I was holding.

Ryan drops his hands and looks away, clearing his throat as he grabs his bag. He gestures for me to walk through the door, and I hurry forward. My pulse still racing as I focus on the source of the commotion, but my mind lingers on the electrifying connection we just shared.

"I welcome you into my home for three minutes and you're already breaking things?" I ask as calmly as I can as I enter the kitchen, looking at a guilty-faced Sam and Dani who are bent over a pile of baking trays on the floor.

"Not breaking!" Sam insists, "just reorganising in search of something else." He puts the trays down carefully on the kitchen island. This is the ideal distraction from whatever that was with Ryan that made my heartbeat so fast.

"What are you looking for, I can probably help?" I love

how Dani and Sam revert to their most childish selves together. It helps me unwind being a part of their playfulness.

"Cupcake tray? We're going to make those fudge cupcakes from Alley Cats," Sam asks. I hold back my internal feeling of stress at the imminent mess this is going to create. I can tidy it up after they leave.

"Is that the cat café?" Dani asks.

"No, it's a bakery," says Sam, handing me back the trays.

"With cats?" Dani continues.

"No, it's-" Sam starts.

"Is there an alley?"

"No."

"I'm hearing a lot of false advertising," says Dani looking disappointed.

"Alright look-" Sam tries again before I interrupt.

"As long as there's baked goods, I'm happy. I'll get you a tray. If you're getting super creative bake a cheesecake next – that's my favourite," I say. Sam loves baking, he's a great cook but an even better baker. I think he finds it quite therapeutic and, like Dani and Leo, he's a massive foodie. Also making things with love and care for other people makes him especially happy, which is a lovely trait of his. I'm expecting him to set up a bakery in retirement just for the love of the game.

I step backwards to get the equipment from under the stairs and unexpectedly press right up against something tall and hard.

Spinning around I realise Ryan is standing right behind me and accidentally hit him in the stomach in the process.

"Oh my god I'm so sorry," I say, backing away into the kitchen island in a panic instead.

He smiles slightly and steps back against the wall, putting his hands in the air in surrender.

"Don't worry, it's my fault."

It definitely wasn't, but I need to focus on finding the cupcake tray right now, and not how incredible it felt being pressed up against him.

A few hours, several burnt cupcakes ("How was I supposed to know that was a grill setting?"), one pub lunch, and an aggressive game of Articulate later, and everyone is settling in for a takeaway and movie.

So far, I had slightly been ignoring Ryan. If I'm being really honest, it's because he makes me nervous. I can't help but gaze at him and I find that everything he says gives me butterflies. I want to sit and talk with him, and gaze into his beautiful eyes. But this will add fuel to the fire, and I can't afford a super big unrequited crush right now. It's currently a medium-large crush, but not super big. That's the next level up.

Especially now that I know he's single. I don't know what that was earlier, but I can't handle any confusing touching. I can't handle looking for a sign, because I'll misread it and assume he likes me when he doesn't.

This is why I tend to lean towards big obvious gestures. I don't do well with ambiguity or a slow burn, it leaves far too much room to assume the worst. I'll just ask if I can kiss you or take you home, so you can accept or reject me up front.

The idea of making a subtle move, or having something build quietly, is completely lost on me.

May says this is why I've never noticed people flirting with me, but I think those people need to be more like me and just ask me out. Like a very mature adult – who is deathly afraid of getting invested and rejected.

"What pairs nicely with losing, pizza and a merlot?" Dani says to Ryan, still holding our winning Articulate piece. We had demonstrated our superior bond over the other pairings with our remarkable win.

"Actually, pizza and beer goes well with modesty, so you guys should probably avoid it tonight," Ryan says back, looking the sassiest I've ever seen him. I love this grumpy, competitive edge coming out.

"The garage is always well stocked with beer. Even if it doesn't go with modesty, it definitely goes with winning so Dani and I are set," I say feeling very smug. I normally play board games with my family who are far more competitive than me, so I typically resign myself to losing. This made a pleasant change. "If I can leave ordering the pizza with you guys, I'll go grab the beer."

"I can help with that," says Leo following me out.

We walk across to the garage and I flip on the light, revealing a mess of garden tools, bikes, and a wheel-less vintage Renault.

"Cute car," says Leo, as I hand him a bag of compost in my quest to reach the beer on the other side.

"Thanks. My Dad bought it for my Mum. It's the same make as the first car she ever owned."

"Wow," says Leo looking impressed, "That's set a good bar for romance. I thought I did well giving Dani the coffee cups she had been eyeing up for our anniversary."

"I mean, you did, those cups are gorgeous," I say, now trying to manoeuvre a wheelbarrow filled with flowerpots, Leo standing a few paces behind ready to be handed the crates.

"Ryan seems to be having a nice time," I say. It feels like a very reasonable thing to say given he's Leo's plus one and new to the group. I'm worried it's obvious I'm too invested. Hopefully Leo doesn't notice.

"Yeah, I think so. I'm glad he fits in well with everyone, or he will once he's more relaxed maybe. I think he's still a bit stressed about trying to make more friends," Leo says, taking the first box of Peronis I hand over to him from my new perch in between a spade and the shelf of drinks.

"I didn't realise he was feeling stressed, he plays it down well. I just thought he was a little quiet," I say, grabbing the second box and starting to *Mission Impossible* my way back.

"I mean he's pretty introverted like me anyway, but sometimes that comes out more when it's the whole group. He's a little quieter than usual," Leo shrugs. "It took me a minute but now I feel super comfortable around you guys, so I'm sure he'll get there."

"Too comfortable, I think" I say, finally extracting myself and standing to face Leo as I lean to switch off the light "You almost beat me and Dani at Articulate, and I can't have that kind of behaviour in my house."

"You're right" Leo says, nodding gravely, "I may be too

comfortable to tell you that you're now covered in cobwebs, and look like a very low budget witch."

Looking down, I can see he's right. This is what happens to the garage when my parents are away for a few days and the spiders settle in at pace.

"Lovely. The price I pay for hosting. I hope you appreciate it," I say, as we walk back to the house, beers in hand.

Stepping inside and putting the crate down on the table, I can see everyone in the corner of my eye debating the pizza selection. Calling to no-one in particular as I walk by, I announce my preference for a margarita or something meaty without sweetcorn, and head upstairs to change.

Hosting can be a lot to manage, but I love having everyone in the house. It creates this cosy buzz being surrounded by such wonderful people who are full of so much joy. It's definitely worth a slightly grim trip to the garage for supplies.

The cobwebs and spiders give me such an ick I can't help but strip as I walk up the stairs, even as I'm smiling to myself hearing everyone chatter away downstairs. Taking my t-shirt off over my head as I turn the corner – I walk right into Ryan. Turns out not everyone was in the kitchen.

We both freeze, suspended in a moment that feels both surreal and electrifying. I stand there with my cobwebbed t-shirt in one hand, now only in my bra and jeans. Normally, I wouldn't think twice about changing in front of friends – I've shared rooms with Sam and Leo on holiday without a second thought. But this feels different, more intimate.

Perhaps it's the way his eyes linger on me, tracing the curve of my waist, making me ache to pull him closer, to feel his hands resting there again.

Finally, his gaze snaps back to mine, and he turns away, flustered. "Shit, sorry."

Reacting instinctively, I throw my t-shirt back on, my cheeks warming as I stammer, "Sorry, I didn't realize you were up here."

"No, it's your house," he replies, still not looking at me.

"True, but you're a guest. Feel free to roam. I just don't usually find myself half-dressed in the corridor."

He laughs lightly, though it's laced with awkwardness. "Yes, well – thank you." I can see him tilting his head, as if questioning whether he should have said anything at all.

"Right…now that I'm clothed again, I just need to scooch past you," I say, shifting cautiously toward him, careful to maintain some distance to avoid another accidental moment.

"Yes, yes, of course… thanks," he replies, his voice tight as he steps aside, looking almost pained by the situation. He hurries down the stairs, leaving me wondering if I should be flattered or embarrassed – or perhaps both.

"You're welcome, I guess?" I murmur to myself, a smile creeping onto my lips despite the awkwardness.

Lying in bed later, I feel restless. Spending two hours that evening sitting next to Ryan was difficult. So difficult I barely enjoyed *Jurassic Park*. I was staring at the TV hardly seeing anything, focusing on not moving. Acutely aware of the fact that our arms were touching side by side for the first hour.

Despite seeing it many times before, I couldn't help but jump slightly when the velociraptors made their deadly move

– which put my hand right next to his. I tried to think it didn't matter, I wouldn't have noticed if it were Dani or Sam's hand, but all I could think about was the tiny connection between my finger and his. It was probably just a centimetre of skin on skin, but it sparked that electricity again. The warm comforting feeling of connection, intertwined with a magnetic energy that made me want to get as physically close to him as I could.

My eyes completely glazed over watching Laura Dern. All I could see was an image of me climbing on top of Ryan and getting as close as physically possible. Putting my hands in his hair while he puts his hands under my shirt. Gently bringing our faces together, moving slowly in time as his hands move against my skin. Grinding together and feeling the heat build between us. Thank goodness no one can tell that my mind is wandering in that direction.

This is ridiculous, I'm trying to be responsible and not fall for men who don't want me. Or to sleep with men I actively dislike, hence my small collection of unread messages from the archived roster. Lying in bed I'm trying to resist the temptation to start opening these messages as a distraction.

If I was in London, I would probably give in. But being in Cambridge, there's no point even looking right now. What am I going to say – "could you get an uber for an hour to my parent's house, sneak in so you don't wake my friends, have sex with me, then leave?" I probably could find someone to take up the offer but it's a bit extreme, even for me.

I need to get out of my head. I'm going to get toast. When I can't sleep and I've already tried my normal bedtime routine of listening to a *Harry Potter* audiobook for 30 minutes, but my brain is still in overdrive, the answer is toast. The small routine of making toast and eating it quietly is enough to take my brain away from whatever is winding it up.

Conscious that it's almost midnight, I quietly step out of bed and head downstairs to the kitchen. I'm not worried about bumping into anyone at this hour, but my oversized Chappell Roan tour t-shirt will have me covered just in case I do. My parents like to run the house very warm so no need for pyjama bottoms despite it being November. Just the reliable M&S-black-no-VPL-high-waisted pants.

Putting the toast in the toaster, I sit on the counter and close my eyes, trying not to let work creep into my head. One of the projects pops up for a split second but I bat it away, forcing myself not to open my eyes to write a next step on my phone. What's worse, thinking about work or a crush? This is what Mr Darcy meant by it being a torment.

Suddenly something touches my shoulder and I jump, swinging my arm up and hitting something solid. Ryan's face. Fuck fuck fuck.

"Oh my god!" I say, as he buckles over holding his nose. "I am so sorry! Oh my god!" I jump off the counter and grab some kitchen roll, tearing it off and holding it up to him. "Are you okay?"

Bit of a silly question after I sort of punched him in the nose.

"Yes, all good," he says, starting to stand up straighter. He takes the kitchen roll to press to his nose which has started to bleed slightly. "Sorry I didn't mean to scare you, I just wanted to get a glass of water."

He tilts his head back with his hands pressed firmly on his nose. I'm momentarily distracted by his neck again and how good it looks and how much I wish my face was brushing against his skin.

"It was completely reasonable, I just had a bad reaction. I was feeling a bit tense so I think my arms went into fight mode," I say apologetically, moving my arms to demonstrate. "Would you still like a glass of water? Or an ice pack? Or an accidental insurance number?"

Ryan moves his hand away and looks at the tissue dotted with blood.

"Maybe just the first two?"

"Least I can do," I say, moving around him to grab a glass from the cupboard behind. Turning around I now see he's wearing a t-shirt and boxers, oh have mercy. His legs look strong and sturdy, like he could just hold you up against a wall for hours without breaking a sweat. This is also giving me a really teasing view of what it would be like to see him in the early mornings, or how it might feel sitting on top of him.

Bringing my eyes back up, I walk to the sink to fill up the glass and grab a pack of frozen peas from the freezer, holding them out to Ryan who takes them with thanks.

We stand quietly for a moment as he breathes a sigh of release into the peas.

"I'm really sorry," I say again. This poor guy who just came to make friends and stay hydrated, instead gets assaulted.

Ryan smiles under the peas, "Don't worry. I should have

known to announce my presence from a distance – like approaching a wild cat or something." He moves the peas away, "How does it look?"

Incredibly gorgeous is my first thought, but I try to focus on the nose.

"Not bad, I don't think it's going to bruise or anything, but there's still a bit of blood on your face." I take a bit of a kitchen roll and wet it in the sink, holding it up to Ryan who seems to be waiting for something, peas in hand.

"Do you mind getting it?" he asks, squinting past his sore nose and gesturing to his face.

"Oh yeah of course," I say, stepping closer.

He puts the peas and glass on the counter, turning back to face me. Very conscious not to let our bodies touch, I move my hand up and start to gently wipe away the blood.

I can feel his eyes on me as I gently dab his cheek. Being so close to him is magnetising. I can't face looking into his eyes while we're so close, so I try to focus on cleaning off the dots of red – and not the smooth shape of his cheek and the dark bristly hair of his stubble.

My arm leans against his chest slightly to steady my hand and suddenly I'm even closer. I feel like I want to melt against him completely and it's taking everything in me to stand still.

"I…think that's all done," I say, starting to move my hand away from his face. We're so close now I have nowhere to put it, so it just hovers over his shoulder. I can't seem to move away.

I can see the light freckles on his cheeks, and I can't help but let my eyes flick up to look into his. Dark brown gemstones with tiny flecks of gold and green bore into me.

It's the sparks again. I'm being drowned in his beauty. It's completely overwhelming. It's like I can't breathe. All I can do is stand and stare.

Slowly yet suddenly, Ryan moves his hand to my waist, grounding me where I've frozen. My hands move gently down to hold his shoulder, like an ivy growing faithfully around an anchoring oak.

As though said by someone else, I hear myself ask, "Can I kiss you?"

Chapter 16. Him.

Dear God. Yes please, is the first thing that comes to mind but instead I just lean forwards and put my lips to hers. It's as tentative and constrained as her question. It's a nervous answer. The minute she starts to lean into the kiss it feels like we're both turning a nervous question into a public declaration.

My hands move instinctively up to touch her face, feeling the softness of her cheek as our faces intertwine, our noses nudging affectionately together. I move one hand into her hair as the other wraps around her waist to pull her gently into me. Every second we kiss I want her closer and closer.

She must feel the same, because as my fingers tighten in her hair, she moves forward between my legs, her body pressing against me as her hips pin me to the counter. Despite bending down to bring my face to hers, she stands on her tip toes to get closer to me, causing her body to press on top of me even more. I desperately want her on me, but in this moment I settle for tightening my grip on her ever so slightly.

In response, her hands drift under the fabric of my t-shirt. Her touch feels completely electric against my skin and the image of her sitting naked on top of me runs through my mind. She moves her fingers softly along my side, pushing gently against my boxers. This combination of full body pressure and teasing soft touches is driving me crazy. I make a mental note to return the favour.

I tilt her face up towards me more so I can kiss her deeper. We're twisting together in an intensely beautiful way.

I feel this burning need to touch her more, my hands drifting across her waist and down slowly to her ass. Touching the soft skin under her underwear, I can't help but groan slightly against her mouth. I'm struggling to think straight. All I can think about now is getting between her thighs.

Without breaking from the kiss, I lean down to lift her up, so her legs wrap around me. As I step forwards to seat her on top of the counter, she pulls away suddenly. Looking slightly panicked, she turns to look around, her hands moving to the surface. Is she checking that it's clear? She can't let someone else run the show for two seconds I swear.

Laughing slightly to myself once she's seated, I can't help but stand back for a second to ask, "Comfortable?"

She looks around again, taking my question much more seriously than I intended. "Yes," she says with a smile.

Smiling back, I lean back into the kiss with a renewed excitement now that I have her where I want. Her hands move naturally around my neck as her legs wrap more tightly around my waist. The way she's holding onto me is intense – like she's been waiting for this forever. Given the way she's been crossing my mind on repeat lately, I know the feeling.

Tangled up together on the counter it feels like everything has moved to slow motion. Her hands in my hair. My arms wrapped around her, pulling her into me. The cold stone of the granite digging into my thighs as I try to stand as close as possible to her. Her hips grinding gently against me, making my brain go haywire and my body feel on fire.

If the breakdown in *Redbone* spun into a tangible moment – it would be right now.

This could go on forever and I would be the happiest man alive. Suddenly something sparks in my brain – what could happen next? Could this go further or does she just want to kiss? What does it mean that we're doing this? Is it a good idea? Feeling her body press against me pushes the other two questions out of my mind but makes the first one even more urgent. I guess I can follow her lead and ask.

"Can I go down on you?" A bit more forward than I was intending, but it's all my brain can come up with right now.

Anna blinks at me, leaning back but still holding onto me so that her hips press flush against mine. "Err I mean um…" she starts, looking flustered.

"I don't have to, don't worry-"

"No, that would be great. Really great," she interrupts. "Sorry I," her hands flail around slightly, "sort of lose my head sometimes and I can't," she flails again, looking across to the wall as if looking for the words, "speak."

I've never seen her so out of control. It's incredibly hot.

Especially knowing I did this.

"Okay, but that's a yes?" I ask. It's incredibly hot but if she's lost her head, I just want to be sure.

"Yes. Definitely, yes. Please," she says, nodding enthusiastically.

She doesn't have to tell me twice, or I guess she did. But now that that's confirmed I've got free rein. My face goes to her neck just below her ear. I hear her make a quiet moan of pleasure which tells me this is going in the right direction. My hands move up her thighs under her t-shirt until my thumbs are on her hips and I start to move down to kiss the base of her neck. Slipping my thumbs into her underwear I gently start pulling them down as she leans back to help me slide them off.

As I'm about to move down to my knees, I look around and step back towards the table at the end of the counter instead.

Anna looks startled again, "Where are you going?"

"Just pulling up a chair," I say, grabbing a chair from the table and seating myself comfortably between her legs. I can't do my best work crouching on a cold floor.

She looks somewhere lost between laughter and excitement, but before she can say another word, I slide my hand under her right leg and put it comfortably over my shoulder as I pull her closer towards me.

I can hear Anna taking shuddering breaths and muttering something to herself as I push up the edge of her t-shirt and gently kiss her inner thighs, letting my stubble rub against her skin ever so slightly. I can just about see her lay back on the counter with her hands over her face as I move my thumb between her legs. For a second I think I should get her something for her head, but feeling how wet she is makes my mind goes blank. I let out a groan of longing in the back of my throat. I can feel her leg shaking slightly on my side as I move my thumb as slowly as I can up and down. Quiet "oh my god's" above me confirm it's having the desired effect.

I can't help but keep the moment going, holding her on the edge like this. Keeping my thumb going slowly, I move my mouth back to her thighs and kiss lines along everywhere I can reach. I can feel her pushing into me in desperation, which feels like an invitation for more. Grabbing one leg with my hand, I rake my teeth gently over the faint marks I've already left, prompting an aggressive line of swearing from above me.

Smiling to myself and unable to resist any longer, I move my tongue in and gently lick as my thumb moves circles slowly at the top. The continuous moans of "oh my god" have progressed to "oh fuck, oh fuck, oh fuck".

I desperately want to be inside her fully but also feel like I could do this forever. The way she sounds and how she feels right now is incredible. Swapping my hand and tongue around I move my thumb down, feeling the soft wet skin and slowly start to tease before sliding it inside. I feel her body shudder and she lets out another broken "oh my god" from above me. I want to kiss her roughly and hold her so tight I leave bruises – but that will have to wait.

Taking my thumb out I move two fingers in, taking slow deep strokes as I trace my tongue around her clit. Looking up

I can see her hands over her face, then one hand moves down and grabs my hair as her back arches up towards me. I can't help but smile out of the corner of my mouth, feeling her pulling my hair.

I grab her thigh with my other hand, pressing tightly against her skin to hold her still. It is so hot seeing how much she's enjoying herself I feel almost on edge myself.

Feeling the intensity build, I start moving ever so slightly faster, keeping a slow steady rhythm until her hand grips my hair almost painfully tight and I feel her whole body shake. Her leg curls up, almost choking me against the edge of the counter as she comes. Good thing I was holding her thighs or it may have been the end for me. But man, what a way to go.

Looking up I can see her with one hand still over her face breathing deeply. As it looks like she may need a moment, I kiss her inner thighs again gently. As I stand, I stroke her legs to help calm her back down.

"Sorry I just…." she starts, in between some heavy breathing, "need a minute."

It doesn't get any better than this, looking at her lying as a happy mess on the counter with her t-shirt tangled up revealing a smooth pale stomach. I move my hand up to her hip and gently stroke with my thumb in time with her shallow breaths. Slowly her breathing seems to slow down to normal.

I really want to kiss her stomach and pull her in to kiss me again, but she still looks a little too overwhelmed. So, I resign myself to stand against the counter between her legs instead, happily enjoying the view.

After another few minutes she pulls her hands away and starts to sit up. "Sorry. Sometimes it's like so good…but so intense. I just need a second."

What a strange thing to feel the need to apologise for. "Not at all, I'm glad you liked it."

She looks at me with her eyebrows raised. "That was amazing," she says seriously. "Like…." She seems to be struggling for words again. She holds up her hand in the 'okay' sign with one finger and thumb pressed together and nods seriously. "Really good."

Her cheeks are still incredibly flushed, and her eyes are hazy. I've never seen her look like this before, a special combination of happy and relaxed. Now I know how to do this, I want to see her like this every day.

She leans back on her hands, exhaling slowly. "Okay, I'm functional again," she says, a smile brightening her face as she looks at me.

Sitting upright, her hands find my shoulders for a fleeting moment, then she pulls them back. She hovers nervously as though she's not sure what to do, eventually resting them on her thighs.

Was this a mistake? It felt incredible, but now a wave of uncertainty washes over me.

I desperately want to kiss her again, to pull her close and hold her tight. But what's going through her mind? Does she want that too? Should I even be considering a relationship right now? I've told myself I shouldn't.

The way her hands just fell away from me suggests she might not be looking for anything more. That realisation hits me like a train.

"Do you want to keep things casual?" I suggest, my voice steady, despite the turmoil inside. The words echo Tom's advice – an escape route. I could spend time with Anna unapologetically. I don't even know what casual really means but I know I can't just back away now; if this is the answer to bridging the gap between friendship and something more, then it's definitely worth it.

"Casual?" she repeats, frowning slightly. "Like, hooking up as friends?"

"Yeah, something like that," I reply, trying to project confidence I don't fully feel. If that's her definition, I can work with it. It also means we're officially friends, which feels oddly comforting, and maybe it'll open the door for more.

"Okay, that could be fun," she says, her shoulders relaxing as she brings her hands back up to my neck. This time, her fingers glide to the back of my head, gently stroking my hair. If I were a cat, I'd be purring.

"Alright then," I say, feeling a mixture of excitement and apprehension. I'm unsure of what comes next or what this all means, but then she leans in to kiss me, wrapping her legs around me and pulling me closer. Her hands weave into my hair, and suddenly I'm lost in the moment, every worry slipping away as our connection deepens.

Chapter 17. Her.

Casual. Friends who hook up. It's a definition I can understand. Is it a bad idea? Maybe. But I think I can do it. From experience I've learned it just requires some careful compartmentalising and self-awareness. You need to keep your eyes open to pinpoint the exact moment feelings start to rear their ugly head.

It works best when you are barely friends. Because if you're friends, the feelings between friendship and romance become blurred and someone may get hurt, normally me.

Ryan and I aren't really friends. We're acquaintances. Do I find him adorable and sweet and beautiful to look at, yes. Do I find myself drawn to him both in my daydreams and reality? I mean of course. It may be a borderline dangerous level of crush, but knowing romance isn't an option makes it easier to just draw a line.

The minute he suggested this, an opportunity opened up

to touch him without worrying what it meant, or how he felt, or what he was thinking. An invitation to be close to him. I couldn't resist it, because holding back from having his skin against mine was absolutely killing me.

We can compartmentalise this into something casual. That's a royal 'we'. I'm just talking about myself. I'm sure Ryan is very happy keeping it casual. The fact he suggested it is a pretty clear sign he doesn't want a relationship with me.

Which is going to be a very important definition to stop me feeling anything more. This could work well for me in the short term. I have been trying to avoid sleeping with people I actively dislike (I think we call that growth?). Instead, I could sleep with someone I actually find pretty great without the risk of it becoming anything more. Perfect.

With work so crazy, this could be the ideal way to have some of the physical benefits without the fear of an emotional investment. It also means I can be all over Ryan in private which is such a gift because touching him is heavenly. Last night in the kitchen, it was like we just fell into place together. I always get self-conscious when someone is going down on me, but he just made it so easy. My god it was good. Whoever he learned that from is owed a written thanks from me.

We didn't get a chance to have sex last night. After my brain had pulled itself back together, we continued kissing. I put my hand in his boxers to get us started again, but before it could go much further, he came. I maybe should have toned down the moaning into his ear, but I couldn't help it. He was apologetic but it feels practically complimentary when someone finishes so soon after getting you off. Glad you were enjoying it too.

Based on our new 'casual' status, going back to his room wasn't necessary. So, we bid each other a friendly goodnight after that.

No goodnight kiss, which went against my instincts to be as physically close to him as possible, but good practice. If I can't handle not kissing him goodnight, I definitely can't handle anything more in the future. I can handle it. I just need to set those boundaries in my head.

Waking up in my bed alone is a good start. It gives a bit of space from last night. We can do it again and it won't mean anything. I can do this. I really want to be able to do this because being with Ryan last night was amazing. Not only because of the incredible kitchen counter action, yes that was top tier, but I felt so calm with him.

I mean, it was a bit stressful when I hit him in the face but being close to him tuned everything else out. I wasn't worried about work or hosting. I was just looking at him and it felt like nothing else mattered. Nothing else existed. Just us in that moment. Which was a peace and calm I'm not really used to. That's worth setting boundaries for.

Hearing the rustlings of people downstairs, I start to get up to join them. After doing a quick teeth and hair brush, and pulling on fresh clothes, I head down. Spotting the corner of the counter where I experienced a heart stopping orgasm last night feels like an exciting secret. But I need to ignore it for now so I don't accidentally blurt it out as breaking news. Ryan and I didn't mention whether we would tell other people, but as it's casual I guess it wouldn't matter?

"Morning!" Sam calls cheerfully from next to the kettle. "I've made madeleines," he says with a joyful smile like it's the most normal way to start a Sunday. The little madeleines look incredibly soft and buttery. It smells like I've just stepped into a French bakery in the countryside.

Sam hands me a madeleine and says, "We're also about to do bacon, eggs, and toast. We found some lone toast in the toaster – do you know if that's from this morning or shall we throw it away?"

I forgot about the toast. I was distracted.

Shaking my head noncommittally I say, "Not sure, just throw it." I am a terrible liar. Got to keep it vague.

"Alrighty," Sam says, throwing the toast away and setting up a round of fresh bread to start toasting.

"Morning Anna, what's your drink of choice?" Stella asks from Sam's side as she opens the cupboard of teas and coffees.

"Coffee please," I say, as Dani and Leo come through the door.

"Ooh wait, I brought my V60!" Leo says, grabbing a bag from the side.

Leo is a coffee nut – if that's an appropriate phrase for it. He is the sort of person to bring their own coffee making kit to other people's homes. The best part is that it means incredible drinks for everyone in the vicinity, and Dani says it makes buying birthday presents really easy. Until you get to surprisingly expensive grinders that is.

Sam steps in to smell the beans as Stella inspects the various bits of equipment. I start filling up a jug of juice when Ryan walks in freshly showered with damp hair. I would pay good money, maybe all my money, to see him fresh out of the shower in a towel. I would commit a crime to acquire more money to pay to see this.

The main travesty of things finishing so suddenly last night was that I didn't get to take his clothes off. Feeling his skin underneath his t-shirt was tantalising, and I've created a very detailed image in my head, but I really want to see the real thing. Imagine him stepping out of the shower, clean and fresh, steaming, water droplets moving down his chest…

"Anna the juice!" Dani says, making me look down at an overflowing jug with juice all over the table.

"Oh shit, my bad," I say quickly. I turn to grab a cloth to start tidying, where I see Ryan already holding out the kitchen roll with a calm smile.

"Definitely need your morning coffee," he says, as Stella takes the pot to the table.

I laugh it off and look away as I finish tidying up.

Somehow, I am dropping Ryan back at Cambridge station. I mean, it was my idea because it made the most sense logistically. Dani, Leo, Sam and Stella all live further across London than me, so they have a longer drive. It's quickest for Ryan to get the train to Kings Cross instead of being driven in. Since I have the shortest drive, I said I could take him to the station first.

I'm so distracted I forget to put on music for the drive before getting in the car, which means *Harry Potter* starts playing aloud as I turn on the engine and my phone syncs up.

Stephen Fry's voice as Fleur Delacour starts speaking out

loudly calling Harry a 'little boy' before I can panic slap the off button.

"Sorry about that," I say, looking sideways to Ryan who looks perplexed, as I realise how close these seats are. Have they always been this close, or has it just been a while since I've been so painfully aware of who's sitting in my passenger seat? "I listen to audiobooks when I go to sleep. It helps distract me and quiets my brain down so I don't get all worked up."

"Worked up from sleep?" Ryan says, as I start pulling out of the drive.

"Yeah, like I just start thinking about things and it can be hard to shut my brain down," I say, I feel like this is maybe a bit personal for my new 'casual' friend, but I have never been good at being a closed book. "Listening to an audiobook, it pulls you away from your own thoughts, gives you something new to focus on to quiet out the noise."

"Makes sense. What's keeping you awake that you need a distraction from?" he asks. I turn to glance at him as we turn round the roundabout, but he's looking curiously out of the window at the cows grazing next to the road.

"Err…anything. Normally work, I can't help but start my to do list for tomorrow. Or I think about things I need to do that I should have done today, or emails I should have sent, or ways to make projects better. There's always too much going on," I say with a laugh, trying to lighten what threatens to become a stressed ramble.

"Sounds exhausting, I'm sorry," Ryan says. When I glance back, he's looking right at me with a slight frown of concern.

"It's fine, I do it to myself. I can't help but take on more work because I see things that need doing and just want to do them. I need to get better at setting boundaries with it. It's not ideal having it on my mind all the time," I say, keeping my eyes back on the road so I don't start getting tempted to lean over on Ryan's shoulder with my eyes closed as I want to right now.

"Anyway, a different thing to think about – this casual thing you said last night," I say, trying to sound casual.

"Er yeah, what about it?" Ryan says, clearing his throat. It's my turn to frown slightly or at least have a puzzled expression.

"Nothing, just checking you were still keen I guess." Not sure what I wanted to ask, just confirmation that last night wasn't a one-time thing? That he still wanted to see me in some way?

"Yeah definitely. If you still want to do something," he says. We're thankfully pulling into the station so this awkward conversation can end soon.

"I'm keen," I say, pulling into a space. I turn to look at him and get momentarily startled by his beautiful eyes looking back at me. "Cool, well we can text to sort something," I say, not sure how else to wrap this up.

"Sounds good. Thanks again for having me this weekend, it really meant a lot," he says earnestly, leaning back to grab his bag and head out. "See you soon." And with a wave, he was gone.

Slumping back in my seat and watching him walk away I feel a pang of longing. I wish he was still sitting with me. I didn't want to risk an emotional conversation which might tip me into feeling something warm and affectionate, so it's probably for the best that he's gone. Something about him makes me want to open up, like there's something comforting about his presence that lets me relax.

I switch to the latest Taylor Swift album to carry me home, but it's not enough of a distraction. Halfway to Islington I'm starting to reel off my to do list for tomorrow. I have a day out on Tuesday for a training session I forgot about, so I need to move all my meetings. I was meant to set up an hour for my team to play boardgames and have snacks because it's been so intense. But that was meant to be on Tuesday and now I'll have to move it back a week. Plus, the feedback from the team was that we should do a listening session instead. Is it wrong to bring snacks to a listening group, or would it help make it more relaxed and encourage open conversation? I need to make sure the manager in my team is okay to cover the governance session, and we were meant to do mid-year review prep which I will also need to push back. And there was pre-work for training, and….

I cut myself off mid-thought to take a breath. It hasn't quite done it. I can feel the anxious energy rattling painfully through my bones against my skin. I fall back on the second best option and yell aloud to myself in the car over Taylor to try and calm down. This spiralling is a problem. Okay, let's focus on the music, focus on the drive, focus on the music. 'The Prophecy' is playing and I don't think I can focus on that right now.

Skipping to my 'Repeat Rewinds' playlist and Craig David

comes on instead. Perfect early noughties escapism. Okay, this is fine. Craig keeps me company until I pull into the garage of my building and turn the car off. My mind is slightly clearer, but my arms still feel like I can barely hold them still. Taking it in turns I tense and flex my hands, trying to push against my muscles and force the energy out. I shut my hands as tightly as possible and dig the remaining short scraps of my bitten nails against my palms.

When this feeling hits, if I don't do something with my body I might just burst at the seams.

Pulling out my phone I scroll down to bring up Ryan's unsaved number and write out a text "Free this week?"

Chapter 18. Him.

"What do you mean you've got a friend coming over for the night?" Nicki asks, leaning against the doorway, arms crossed, a mischievous grin on her face.

I'm in the middle of tidying my room, though it's already pretty neat. Still, I find myself questioning the strategic placement of every single item.

"Just like I said, I have a friend coming over," I reply, shifting a few books from my desk to the shelves.

"Yes, but you said it like it's a secret. You haven't had any friends over before and as I far as I can tell you only have two, Leo and Dani, and if it was them, you would just say. It's 9pm on a Wednesday, which is a bizarre time for a friend to visit. And you're acting like they're staying the night. Is it someone from home?" Nicki presses, raising an eyebrow.

I start to resent how well she knows me.

"Aren't flatmates in big cities supposed to be strangers

who send passive-aggressive texts about dirty dishes? Not detectives who can read my every weird habit," I say frustrated. "How come you're in anyway? I thought Alex had that thing with his football friends today?"

Nicki doesn't reply straight away, prompting me to turn and look at her. She's normally the most talkative person in any room so a moment of silence is concerning. She suddenly looks almost as nervous about something as me.

"Er…yeah I decided to stay home tonight. Have a quiet one," she says, in a way that tells me this isn't the whole story.

"Is everything okay?" I ask, concerned.

Nicki looks up and smiles at me in a reassuring way. "Not really, but it's fine. I just wanted some time at home tonight, not with a swarm of lads in a pub."

"Okay…do you want to talk about it?" I say.

"Not right now – but thanks," she says, looking a little more relaxed. Even if she doesn't want to talk about it now, I feel like admitting there's something bothering you can be the biggest step to working through it.

Before I can offer another line of support she jumps in again, "And anyway – this isn't my big night, it's yours. And you still haven't told me who's coming over? Don't think you can use your charming customer service schmoozing to make me forget."

"Well, this is a new friend. The girl I organised the engagement party with. Dani's best friend," I explain, feeling the heat rise in my cheeks as I debate whether to stash away my illustrated *Lord of the Rings* books. Do I look like a nerd? Should I hide them, or should I leave them out to show I have interests? And who knows if she'll actually stay over? It feels too late for her to just pop in and pop out, right? Or is that what usually happens?

"Wait, so it's a date? That's why you're tidying up?" Nicki's eyes sparkle with excitement.

I stand up, clutching a book in each hand, feeling like a deer caught in headlights. "It's not a date. We're friends. It'… casual," I say, trying to project an air of nonchalance, but Nicki's sceptical look tells me I'm not convincing anyone.

"How very *Sex and the City* of you! Nice to see you embracing London life," she teases, stepping back out of the doorway. "If it's really casual, I wouldn't stress about hiding your hardcore nerd books, but maybe throw on a fresh pair of boxers and you'll be golden."

Sighing, I set the books back down. She does have a point.

I quickly strip out of my clothes from the day and just as I crack open my drawers to change, the doorbell rings. Great. I'm either late, she's early, or a helpful combination of both, and here I am, about to be caught naked in my own room.

"Your future wife is here!" Nicki calls out, her voice echoing as she bounds down the stairs. Glad she's feeling a bit perkier already, but I really hope the sound doesn't travel all the way to the front door.

Quickly throwing on my clothes, I hear muffled conversation from downstairs and rush to the landing. There's Anna, standing in the same long, dark purple skirt she wore to the engagement party. She looks fantastic. Nicki and Anna seem engrossed in a lively discussion, like old friends catching up, so I hang back on the stairs for a moment.

"I mean, I love that it's a fully vegan menu, but sometimes you just need real scrambled eggs, you know?" Anna says, looking composed and relaxed, her hands animated as she speaks. Nicki nods in agreement.

"And frankly, a vegan croissant just can't compare to a fully buttered almond one," Nicki chimes in, her tone matter-of-fact. Anna nods back vigorously, her hands gesticulating to emphasize her point. Then she turns to me and smiles, a warm "Hey" lighting up her face.

"Hey," I reply, still hovering on the stairs, unsure whether to squeeze onto the landing or let them continue. Thankfully, Nicki makes the call for me, declaring, "I better get back to *Made in Chelsea*. Nice meeting you, Anna! I'm glad Ryan's met someone who appreciates Acre Lane bakeries as much as I do."

As she passes me, Nicki leans in and whispers, "Your t-shirt is inside out, stud." Great. Just what I need.

Hopefully, Anna won't notice as she slips off her boots and turns back to me with an expectant smile. "Lovely flat! Can I have a tour?" she asks, glancing toward the open kitchen.

"Of course," I reply, gesturing for her to lead the way. As she steps inside and pauses, I linger in the doorway, uncertain of my next move. She spins around slowly, examining the pictures on the wall, then looks back at me. "It's funny being in your kitchen after watching you cook in it, it feels like stepping onto a film set."

"Although most film sets don't have their flatmate's laundry strewn in the corner," I say, nodding toward the pile of Nicki's sports bras on the clothes horse by the fridge.

Anna laughs, and the sound eases some of my nerves. Maybe this won't be so awkward after all.

"Probably not," Anna agrees, walking slowly towards me. I stand up straighter on instinct, unsure what to do next. Do we just start kissing?

Anna smiles at me expectantly, "Can I see the rest of it?" she says.

Ah yes, the flat tour that she asked about two minutes ago. Watching her stand in front of me had completely stopped my train of thought.

I step back to let her pass me on the stairs, which also gives an incredible view of her ass in this skirt. We step into the lounge where Nicki is happily seated on the sofa.

"Our lounge and work from home set up," I say, pointing to our desks on the side, "That's Nicki's room, and my room is up there," I say, pointing to the next set of stairs.

"It's a gorgeous space, so nicely decorated," Anna says, looking appreciatively at the open shelves covered in books, photos, and fairy lights.

"Thanks," says Nicki loudly from the sofa without looking over.

Anna starts walking upstairs to my room. After a brief pause, I follow her up, hovering in the doorway again as she stands and looks around.

"Nice room," she says, leaning over the desk to inspect the shelves. "Wow, these are incredible!" She lifts the illustrated *Lord of the Rings*, her eyes sparkling with interest. "I've seen these for *Harry Potter*, but not for *Lord of the Rings*. They're beautiful. Do you have a favourite part?"

I'm surprised at her excitement around *Lord of the Rings*, but glad that leaving the books on display turned out to be a good thing. I step closer, my heart racing a little as she flips through the pages. "Rivendell, definitely. Look at this." I gently place my hands over hers to guide her to the right section near the beginning. We pause on an illustration of a balcony, light streaming in and plants spilling over the edges, creating a serene oasis bathed in a soft golden glow.

"Beautiful choice," Anna says, studying the page intently. "What do you love about it?"

"I don't know," I reply, caught off guard by her question. Trying to ignore the feeling of her hand under mine, and her arm gently pressed against my chest as we stand so close together. "It feels so special, yet so real. It's this ancient place full of magic, but you could find that kind of magic in a forest in Germany. The woods near where Leo and I grew up remind me of this. There's a lot of secret beauty in the everyday, if you look for it."

I'm surprised by my own words. I've never considered why that image resonates with me so deeply until now. But as I say it, I realise it's a reminder to seek out the quiet peace in everyday life, to find those moments that make you feel most yourself. The places and the people that make you feel most at home.

Anna looks up at me, her expression thoughtful. "I get that," she replies softly. "Sometimes it's the little things that hold the most magic."

Her understanding sends a warm ripple of connection

between us. I feel the tension easing, replaced by a shared appreciation for those fleeting moments of beauty that can change everything.

I turn from the page to look back at Anna who is still looking up at me. Her eyes look soft and calm in the evening light. She closes the book and leans towards me, putting one hand on the side of my face and kisses me. I take the book out of her hand and put it down behind me, pulling her in close, feeling the soft silk of her skirt under my hand as I give myself free rein to touch her. Unable to hold back, I push her back onto the bed and move on top of her.

It feels electric being tangled up together. Her skirt is soft and rises up easily so that my hands are on her thighs in seconds just as I imagined. Before I can move any further, she flips me onto my back and straddles me. She takes off her top, showing the same lace bra I saw in Cambridge and have been thinking about every day since. Sitting up I move straight into her neck, holding her tightly with one arm while the other continues moving up her thigh. She lets out a moan I will be replaying in my dreams, then pushes me back again and starts moving down to take off my jeans.

I take a calming breath, desperate for things to last longer this time. It's hard when you haven't had sex with anyone for months, and then someone comes in and completely blows your fantasies out of the water.

Sometime later I'm lying on my back trying to return to my senses after the most incredible sex of my life. I had been dreaming about what it might be like for days, getting her legs around me properly, not just around my neck. It somehow surpassed expectations.

Turns out her enthusiasm isn't limited to planning social events. Combined with a very hot level of skill and flexibility, I'm just trying to keep as many of the memories in my mind as I can before they slip away.

There was also this moment where time seemed to slow for a second. Just before I finished, our faces were millimetres apart, our lips almost touching. I'm trying to wrap my head around it, in my dazed state. It felt special, like a real connection, even just for a second. Maybe it was just the effect of being so close to her.

Finally opening my eyes, I see Anna lying naked on her front by my side, propped up on her elbows looking at me. Blinking like she's been caught out, she smiles quickly then turns to look back around my room.

"You have a really nice setup here," she says, glancing around.

"Thanks," I reply, instinctively letting my fingers trail softly along her back, my eyes drifting down to the soft curve at the end of her spine. "You're actually the first guest I've had over. I haven't even had a chance to invite Leo round yet."

"Have you not been dating since you moved here?" Anna asks, her question catching me off guard. It feels too intimate to discuss while we're still lying naked together. I pull my hand back from her, resting it on my chest.

"Not really," I say, trying to downplay it from a more dramatic "Not at all." "My ex and I broke up a few months ago, so now I'm just trying to settle into London."

"I'm sorry. That sucks," Anna replies, her tone softening as she lays her head on her hands, looking at me with those long lashes. "How long were you together?"

"Seven years."

Her eyebrows shoot up in surprise. "Wow, that's a long time."

"Yeah. It's definitely taking some adjusting," I admit, the honesty feeling strangely liberating.

"That makes sense. My ex and I were together for three years, and even that – not having him around felt like a huge shift. You just have to give yourself time," she says with a reassuring smile, stretching slightly like a content cat.

"What about you? Are you dating?" I ask, even though a part of me hesitates. I'm not sure I want to know if she's seeing anyone else, but my curiosity gets the better of me.

"Also not really," she replies, a hint of a wince crossing her face. "I've been putting myself out there this year, but it's been pretty draining. With work being so crazy right now, I don't think I have the headspace to date properly." She shrugs, but I sense there's more beneath her relaxed words.

I can't help but feel a rush of relief knowing she isn't dating other people. This moment, this connection, feels special, something I don't want to share with anyone else.

"Good," I say, my voice steady despite the flutter of nerves. "I mean, that makes sense too. If it's the right thing for you. And…I like this, it's nice… being with you."

Her smile widens, and I can see the warmth in her eyes. "Me too."

I slip into the bathroom, and when I return, I find Anna curled up on her side, fast asleep in my t-shirt – still stylishly inside out from earlier. She looks so peaceful, a gentle smile gracing her lips as she breathes deeply under the duvet. A wave of warmth washes over me; I'm glad she's staying. The thought of her leaving has been painful.

I switch off the light and carefully navigate around the bed, trying not to disturb her as I climb in on the other side. It's a bit of a challenge with the bed pushed against the wall, but I manage to slide under the duvet without a sound.

Once settled, I lay on my back, hands resting on my chest, a mix of contentment and longing coursing through me. Everything in me aches to turn onto my side, to pull her close, to bury my face in the nape of her neck and let my fingers trace the soft curve of her stomach. I can almost breathe in the familiar scent of flowers that lingers around her.

But knowing how stressed she's been, and how much she struggles to sleep, I really don't want to wake her. Instead, I close my eyes, allowing myself to sink into the comfort of sleep, the room filled with the quiet rhythm of her breathing.

Waking up to my alarm feels oddly gentle this morning, a soft intrusion rather than a jarring wake-up call. I reach out to turn it off with one arm, only to discover my other arm is blissfully trapped. Glancing down, I find Anna nestled against my chest, one arm draped over me and her hand resting softly on my heart. The morning light spills into the room, casting a golden glow on her skin, making her look ethereal. As she stirs, I can't help but curse my alarm for breaking this peaceful moment. I wish I'd woken earlier to savour this.

She curls up slightly, then props herself up on one elbow, resting her chin in her hand as she blinks sleepily at me.

"Morning," she says, her smile hazy, but radiant and contagious.

"Good morning," I reply, feeling a warmth spreading through me. She lowers her head to lay on my chest again, taking her time to wake, her hand sliding back down and resting on my side.

I gently graze my fingers up and down her arm, relishing the quiet intimacy between us. I haven't experienced anything like this since Karina and I broke up. I had almost forgotten how nice it can be, lying so close with someone you care about.

Thinking about those moments with Karina, it strikes me for a second how special this feels with Anna. This is only the third time we've been together, just the two of us, and yet it seems so natural. Normally it takes me a lot longer to feel so comfortable with someone.

Even the slightest touch of her hand on my side seems to send something warm through me, like the wind rustling the leaves of a tree, the branches dancing together softly in the breeze.

Anna starts to stretch, prompting me to stop my train of thought. She sits up and glances at me. "I should get up and roll out," she says, beginning to rise.

"Yeah, of course, me too," I reply, taken aback by her sudden movement. Sitting up to follow her, I pause, captivated as she stands and slips off my t-shirt. The sight of her makes my heart race; I want nothing more than to pull her back into bed and keep her there all day, my hands tracing her curves, leaving a map of fingerprints on her thighs.

As she reaches for her clothes, I catch a glimpse of the tattoo I first noticed at the bar, a striking Greek statue on her shoulder. My gaze travels to another tattoo on her side, which resembles a bouquet of flowers, vibrantly growing up her ribcage. Just as I'm lost in thought, she turns to me, breaking my reverie to hand me my t-shirt.

"Sorry, I thought it would be okay to borrow it as pyjamas," she says with a smile.

"Yeah, of course," I manage, trying to hold her gaze. She turns back to put her clothes on and heads to the bathroom, leaving me to lay back in bed, trying to capture this moment in my mind. The gentle morning light, the artistry of her tattoos, her skin glowing softly.

When she returns, I realise I've been completely still, a sense of longing filling the room without her. "What's your tattoo on the side? If you don't mind my asking," I say, sitting up again, curiosity piqued.

"I don't mind," she replies, climbing back onto the bed to lift her top and bra on the side, revealing the intricate design. "It's a collection of flowers, each one representing an important woman in my life. There's an orchid for Dani, a tulip for May, my flatmate, a snowdrop for my best friend from primary school, and something for my mum."

As she speaks, I reach out instinctively, my fingers brushing against the delicate patterns of flowers and leaves intertwined on her skin. I fight the urge to wrap my arms around her and pull her back to me.

"The one on my back is a caryatid, one of those women who holds up ancient buildings and temples," she continues, lifting her top again. "It's for my friend Meg, she's equally museum-obsessed and has a matching one. She always wanted one, and I wanted something with her. It's for all the women whose shoulders we stand on, the weight of being a woman in the world."

"They're really cool," I say, touched by the thoughtfulness behind her tattoos.

"Thank you," she responds, her smile brightening the room. She stands up, gathering her things. "I better be off. Thanks for having me, it was great."

I start to rise to walk her out, but she gestures for me to stay. "Don't worry, I can find my way out," she says, already picking up her bag.

And just like that, she was gone.

Chapter 19. Her.

The night at Ryan's was absolutely amazing. The sex was incredible, but the most wonderful part was just being around him. It was fun to see his room, to glimpse the little pieces of him that make him who he is. Listening to him talk about the things he loves was unexpectedly captivating. I found myself leaning in, unable to resist the urge to kiss him. In that moment, I could feel my heart begin to melt, and it was both thrilling and terrifying.

He invited me to come over again a few nights later, and despite the chaos of work that had me running late, I was determined to make it. When I finally arrived, everything felt just as magical as before. Being with him is like stepping into an enchanted space where it's just us, where nothing else matters and the outside world fades away. It's like he's brought a secret slice of Rivendell to South London just for me.

I'm already counting down the days until I see him again. This time together is helping me navigate the craziness of work, allowing me this special moment of calm. With Ryan, even though we barely know each other, somehow I feel so much more myself.

It's now Saturday night in mid-December. May and I are hosting a themed cocktail night as a 'pre-Christmas' social before everyone heads home for the holidays. The theme is 'Make A Cocktail Based On Your Ex'. My idea.

We're with the motley crew, Dani, Leo, Sam, and Stella. I did tell Leo he was welcome to extend the invite to Ryan, but apparently he had to work. Although I am desperate to see him again, I am slightly relieved. We haven't seen each other in a social setting since Cambridge. I don't know how to spend time together as just friends when I know how incredible it feels being so much more. I'm sure I can find a way through, but it's probably for the best putting the idea in practice when there is no alcohol involved.

We're all sitting around our dining table. Dani is next to the speakers to keep on top of the playlist. She's loyally adding every requested noughties pop hit to the queue on demand, currently playing through a few select Dizzee Rascal hits. The table is already cluttered with various half-drunk rounds of cocktails. Unsurprisingly the theme prompted some extremely creative concoctions – but not necessarily delicious.

"Alright, May, it's your turn!" Stella calls out as we finish the last of our 'Elderflower Collins,' a tribute to Dani's very British ex-boyfriend. May springs into action, striding confidently to the kitchen. The open kitchen-dining-living space is perfect for hosting like this, everyone can stay together in one buzzy group no matter what you're up to.

A few minutes later, she returns with a tray of vibrant shots, interrupting an intense debate between Sam and me about the feasibility of sharing a ranch in the countryside, I would keep horses, he would have a serene escape.

Dani peers suspiciously at the shot glasses as May distributes them. "I'll be brave and ask: what exactly is this?"

"It's an American Shooter," May announces, gesturing proudly at the red, white, and blue layers. "To commemorate my years in Texas with a Michigan man."

"Cheers to happy times!" I say, raising my shot nervously.

May glances at her creation with a hint of concern. "We didn't have all the right ingredients, so I had to improvise a bit."

Sharing a resigned look with Sam, we down the shots, nearly choking on something halfway through.

"Was that meant to be a shot or an entrée? It's going down like a lumpy lead balloon," Sam coughs, his eyes wide.

"I didn't know the Baileys would react like that!" May grimaces, wrinkling her nose in distaste as Dani and Stella burst into laughter.

Next up is Sam's 'Angry Canadian' cocktail, a nod to his ex-girlfriend from the Great White North.

"This really highlights how international our dating pool is," I comment, accepting the glass from Sam.

"Just part of the occupational hazard of living in London," he replies, as everyone begins their next round.

Dani takes a sip and splutters, "Is this just whiskey with a cherry in it?"

"I followed the recipe exactly! This is how it's supposed to taste...I think," Sam defends, valiantly attempting to finish his drink as he grimaces, like a baby tasting lemon for the first time.

The buzzer goes off, interrupting the fresh round of mockery. Looking around the table of confused faces, Leo says, "Oh I forgot to say – Ryan can come tonight."

"Oh great!" I say, springing up to get the door. Great! Kind of! Also panic!

"Does he know about the theme? He will obviously have to make a round?" May says, getting up to follow me.

I press the buzzer to let him in and turn to find May standing behind me. "I realise we have maybe 30 seconds but how are you feeling about having him over?" She asks.

While I didn't know how to tell Dani about Ryan yet, May knew all the drama to date. It's flatmate privilege. She's basically my wife, so more like spousal privilege. I'm not expecting anyone to question my relationship with Ryan in a court of law, but it's nice to feel like the protection is there just in case.

It's also helpful getting a second perspective. I don't always trust my judgement, and May's 'straight to jail' approach to partners means I can be extra careful.

"Good, I think? Or fine at least. It'll be fine. It's nice he can join. I just need to keep my distance, so it doesn't become...coupley. Just got to get through this evening." I say, trying to think on my feet as to how to keep my head when I am so drawn to him. I need to keep it friendly and casual. Ignore how it feels when we're together. How good it feels having his hands on me, and how happy I feel when he smiles.

"Sounds very sensible." She says, "Let me know if you need anything okay?"

"Thank you," I say as I hear a knock on the door. Walking over I let Ryan in. I am star struck at how beautiful he looks. He's wearing a big coat and a knitted hat, his cheeks slightly flushed from the cold. It looks like he's stepped off a skating rink or just finished walking around a Christmas market. I can't help picturing doing these things with him for a split second as he stands in the doorway. The two of us holding hands and laughing together.

I just want to put my hands on his neck and kiss him. I can't do that tonight. Just got to get through this evening.

"Hey, welcome!" May says, "nice to see you again."

"Nice to see you too," says Ryan, as May pulls him into a hug. He then turns to me and goes in for a hug. He feels amazing, even through a big knit jumper.

"Glad you're embracing the British hug habit," I say with a smile as he takes off his shoes.

May starts briefing him on the evening cocktail theme and the clear expectation he will need to make one too. "Think about your terrible exes!" she says, as I start walking back to the lounge to lead him through.

"I don't think I have any?" he says, walking behind me. Of course he doesn't.

Dani slides up to say hello and informs me that it's my turn to cocktail, which works well so I can keep my distance from Ryan for now. I let the happy chatter blend into the Pitbull blazing from the speakers as I prepare my drink and bring the first two glasses to the table.

"Botanical gardens surely? It's a pretty special spot?" Sam is saying as I hand a glass over, moving his hands so animatedly he almost knocks Stella's drink off the table.

"Hey, Leo and I had Rotherhithe Museum. That is so much more niche!" Dani says.

I lean back to the kitchen to grab the next glasses. "What are we debating?" I ask.

"Most unusual places," says May with thanks as I pass her a glass.

"Rotherhithe Museum, really?" I say with surprise and impressed recognition of Dani and Leo's adventurous sexual prowess.

"What about you? Anywhere truly unique?" Leo says.

I pause to think for a second. "I reckon either an office or a train." I say, looking up from setting down the next round of glasses to see some extremely blank faces.

"An office? Who has that kind of connection to work like that?" Sam asks in a sceptical tone.

"Less of an active choice, more of a very boozy Halloween party. I mean I know it's not as wild as a museum, but it's still pretty high stakes," I say to justify myself.

Sam and Dani start laughing, making me frown in confusion.

May puts her hand on my arm and says, "Most unusual place you've been to for a wedding." Prompting the rest of the table to burst into laughter.

Of course, that other classic discussion point of unusual places….why did my brain completely miss the romance?

"Yeah, er, that's what I meant…" I say, looking at my glass and trying to ignore the continued snorts of laughter around me.

"A train really?" Leo says. "Isn't that kind of grim?"

"You know, sometimes inspiration just strikes," I say, acutely aware of the heat creeping up my cheeks. "So, speaking of happy memories and way too much sharing, I've concocted a cranberry margarita with a splash of Fireball. It's red to commemorate all the red flags I missed." This earns me a few chuckles as I finally take a seat next to Sam.

"All the red flags you missed?" Ryan asks, taking a sip and locking eyes with me. I try to ignore the mortification bubbling beneath the surface, wishing he hadn't caught my earlier anecdotes. And how beautiful his eyes look gazing kindly at me over the table.

"Yeah, after my last breakup, I had a bit of a revelation about the obvious signs I overlooked." I launch into a familiar spiel, hoping it masks my embarrassment.

"It's hard to focus on the troubles when you're busy having sex on trains," Leo comments calmly, sipping his cocktail as if we were debating local politics, not my sex life. I shoot him an unimpressed glare.

"Ooh, like that time he made you apologize for upsetting him after you cried!" Sam chimes in, clearly enjoying this.

"Or when he told you your taste was 'just a bit basic'?" Dani adds, a gleeful grin spreading across his face.

May looks a bit concerned, as if we shouldn't be

trivialising these experiences. But I appreciate being able to reframe them as entertaining stories from my past rather than lingering traumas. I'm grateful I'm not in that relationship anymore, so I can laugh about it.

"No, come on, we've got to dig up a hard hitter! My absolute favourite, saved for a special story time. Settle in, kids!" I say, taking a hearty gulp of my drink, deliberately avoiding Ryan's gaze.

Everyone shuffles closer, Dani and Sam linking arms and leaning on each other like toddlers.

"Long story short, at this point, we weren't officially together. It was still early dating days. I call him when I'm really upset – almost crying, wanting to talk to him. He says he shouldn't be the person I lean on for support, hangs up on me. Where was I, you ask? Oh, just at my grandma's funeral," I say, prompting the usual gasps and disappointed groans of disbelief. Everyone bursts into polite applause except for Ryan, who looks slightly disgusted, and May, who pats my arm sympathetically.

"Being put down at your grandma's funeral. You're right, that's a good one – if by 'good' you mean 'really, really bad,'" Leo remarks, shaking his head.

"Arguably more embarrassing because we weren't even in a relationship yet. And in that moment, I thought, 'Yes, this is the man for me,'" I say, trying to maintain a light tone.

"A lesson in keeping an eye out for red flags in the future," May says, smiling kindly at me.

"I don't mean to be rude, but…why were you with him?" Stella tilts her head, genuinely trying to understand my choices.

"It's a fair question when you hear only the bad stuff, but he did make me really happy! You know, it could be great. Our song was 'Love is Easy,'" I say apologetically, momentarily lost in a flashback of belting out McFly in the car as we drove through Sicily.

"And what's your song for him now?" Dani asks, feigning innocence as she leans in to hear my answer.

"…'Oscar Winning Tears,'" I admit, downing the last of my drink.

"There you go," Dani says with a triumphant smile.

"Anyway, on that cheerful note, Ryan, I think you're up next."

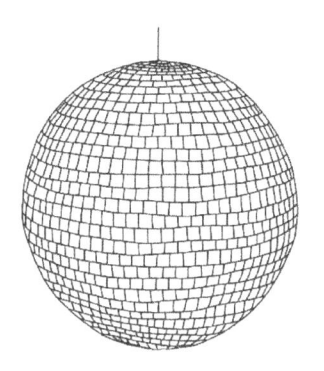

Chapter 20. Him.

Still slightly in awe of Anna's story, and the other *Cliff's Notes* stories shouted from the sidelines, I get up and make my way to the kitchen. Karina and I had problems to be sure, but I can't imagine her doing something like that.

As I walk over, I'm momentarily struck by how inviting this space is, comfortably hosting six very excited and noisy friends. Everyone is scattered around the table, with Dani and Leo at the end, sitting in front of an impressive set of speakers. A large wall of glass behind them reveals a glimpse of London's stars – the dots of hundreds of windows lit up in the surrounding buildings. In the absence of a clear dark sky, I've learned to find beauty closer to home.

Looking back to the kitchen counter, I start to survey the available ingredients. Spotting some tequila on the side, plus some lime and chillis in the fruit bowl gives me an idea. The kitchen is completely overflowing with glasses and liquors, so

I search for some clean instruments.

"Need a hand?" A cheerful voice calls from my side.

I turn to see Anna leaning against the counter, looking radiant in the same blue jeans she wore the first night we met. The mustard yellow vest under her colourful cropped shirt brings out her playful spirit. She looks joyful and flushed, and I can't help but smile.

"Clean glasses?" I ask.

She makes a sceptical noise and steps back, throwing her arms wide to indicate the chaos around us. "You're being way too ambitious there."

"Any glasses?" I reply, chuckling. Anna's already gathering a few and tossing them into the sink, giving me an unobstructed view of her ass in those jeans. I try to refocus on the ingredients in front of me instead of where I wish my hands could be.

"So, what are you making?" she asks, her voice cutting through the cheerful chatter from the table.

"Spicy margarita," I say, squeezing the last of the lime into a bowl.

"May I ask why?" Anna glances back at me, and I have a sudden urge to step up behind her, press her against the counter, lean over her shoulder, and turn her face to mine. Hold her hands down so she can't move.

Instead, I resign myself to standing beside her, drying the freshly washed glasses.

"I haven't had that many relationship dramas, but it felt fitting for my ex. Seems like a great idea at the time, but in hindsight we should have called it a night way earlier," I explain, placing the clean glasses down with a light clink.

Anna tilts her head, a half-serious, sympathetic smile playing on her lips. "You're very brave."

"I like to think so." The moment stretches between us, our eyes locked as the familiar scent of flowers and apricots wafts in from her hair. Just as I start to lean closer, a shout from across the room breaks the spell.

"You have thirsty patrons waiting!" Sam says.

Anna smiles at me then moves quickly back to the table. I return to fill up the glasses, adding lime with a flourish before carrying them over. Everyone grabs their drinks with enthusiasm, diving straight into the fun without a second thought to the cocktail backstory as Jason Derulo blares from the speakers.

I tear my eyes away from Anna, feeling a swell of gratitude to be part of this lively scene. The joy and camaraderie radiating from everyone is heartwarming. Sipping my drink, I settle in next to Sam.

"Is this a standard Saturday night for you guys?" I ask, trying to ignore Anna laughing across the table at May, making my heart skip a beat.

"Oh yeah, house every weekend. Actually, every weekday as well. The long work hours are a cover for the party life," Sam says with a playful smile.

"Adds up." I say, returning his smile. "Have you had the chance to do anything else this week? Or is it just non-stop drinking?"

"Non-stop drinking doesn't stop me from doing other things? You clearly haven't met many English people yet.

Absolute animals the lot of us," Sam says, still maintaining his serious yet sarcastic smile. I'm struggling to keep up. With the jokes, and the alcohol.

"Just kidding," he adds, clearly taking pity on me. "Dani and I were bouldering this morning near Mile End, followed by a bakery run. East London is absolute gold dust for local bakeries."

"Sounds cool. I've never been bouldering, I don't think?" I say with a frown. "I'm picturing running over giant rocks but that doesn't seem right."

Sam laughs at me, "I think you're thinking of fell-running. Bouldering is a bit more like rock climbing, but if you can run over the boulder routes I'll be super impressed." He says. "You should come with us next time we go. You're in South London right? It's not that far from our usual spots."

"That would be fun, yeah. Thanks," I say happily, once again touched by how welcoming everyone is.

Leo turns towards us from the seat over, "Be careful Ryan. One day you don't know what bouldering is, the next you're trying to hang off a door frame because it looks like a challenging V2."

"One to work on – we're yet to convince Leo to join us," Sam says conspiratorially, putting one hand up to hide Leo's face. "And a door frame would never be a V2."

Dani suddenly leans over the table towards us, half jumping out of her seat as she says, "Are you talking about climbing routes?"

Laughing, Sam gently pushes Dani back to her seat across the table, "Yes but if we continue, I think Leo may break up with all of us so let's save this for when we induct Ryan to the boulder lifestyle next weekend."

Dani starts clapping excitedly, already making a WhatsApp group with Sam and me and brainstorming a good chat name.

Leo leans back towards me to catch up on our weeks as the music blares louder and we make our way through the remaining half-drunk cocktails on the table.

WhatsApp group made, Dani has now enticed Anna up to dance dramatically, drink in hand. They launch into an epic interpretive dance that feels straight out of a movie. Stella and May cheer them on from the sidelines, adding to the chaos. I'm trying my hardest not to get distracted by the exposed patch of soft skin above Anna's jeans, spending all my energy staring intently into Leo's face.

Suddenly, Sam announces that he doesn't think Dani can still pull off her party trick, doing sit-ups while wrapped around someone's front. This apparently requires either Leo or Anna to demonstrate, given their reputed leg strength. Leo shrugs and stands up, ready to oblige. I finish my drink, feeling less like an outsider with each passing moment.

Dani proves she still has the core strength of a 21-year-old, effortlessly doing several sit-ups on Leo while the room erupts in applause. It's heartwarming to see how everyone here flows together so effortlessly, yet they extend that warmth to newcomers like me.

After a few rounds of a British drinking game called 'King Cup,' which evokes a delightful wave of nostalgia among the Brits, Anna declares that it's time to shut down the party and head out. She starts ushering everyone out, her energy infectious.

"Where are we going?" I ask Stella.

"Ballie Ballerson," she says, like it's the most obvious thing in the world. I know clubs have edgy names, but this one sounds particularly strange.

We make our way out of the flat in continued noisy chaos and start walking across Haggerston Park. I fall in step with May who is still holding a big red plastic cup of something.

"Limoncello. My journey juice, absolute number one priority. Although this is a bit of an ambitious cup size. I normally just bring a shot, but Anna filled this for me so there you go," she says to me with a laugh, noticing me looking at her hand.

"Sure," I say, nodding in approval.

"So, are you enjoying London life?" May asks, taking a sip of her 'journey juice' as we stroll past a row of charming houses and bustling pubs.

"I love it, especially on nights like this," I reply genuinely, my smile widening as I catch a glimpse of Anna skipping alongside Dani. It's a delightful sight. Anna's height makes it a challenge for her to keep in step with the petite Dani, but this completely impractical attempt only seems to make them laugh more.

I look back at May, only to find her watching me with a curious expression. My heart races, and I quickly avert my gaze, clearing my throat.

Our conversation flows to May's work and her deep love for the theatre, making me realise I should definitely explore that side of London more. She shares wild stories about her office life, filled with more drama than I think I've ever encountered outside of work, let alone with colleagues. She also delegates her cup of 'journey juice' to me.

My initial dignified German sipping is overruled by May after I suggested I may not finish it.

She stops in her tracks and turns to me, chanting like we're at a football match, "We like to drink with Ryan, cause Ryan is our mate…"

Within a few notes the whole group had run back to stand around me.

"And when we drink with Ryan…" they all continued enthusiastically, clapping along.

"Is this when I get initiated into the cult?" I ask, looking puzzled at the cup in my hand. I may be a few drinks down, but I'm very conscious that we're still standing in a residential street near the park.

"He gets it down in 8…7…6…" the cult members continue loudly.

Message received. I finish off the rest of the cup in no time, eliciting cheers. I don't know what Limoncello is, but it's delicious. It reminds me of those spritzers we have in summer at home, but feels like it may pack a bit more of a punch.

When we finally arrive at Ballie Ballerson, I'm greeted with a sight that's both absurd and captivating. A club complete with dance floors and bars, but also two enormous ball pits – as in, the thing for children.

If you had asked me whether a ball pit was a good idea for

adults, I would have said no. Surely it would be like sitting in sand, not exactly thrilling. But within moments of diving in, I'm sold. The sheer joy of everyone leaping in and out, laughter echoing around us, draws me in. I find myself tangled in a playful wrestling match with Leo while Dani and May bombard us with balls.

After the ball pit – what a bizarre phrase for someone in their early 30s – we transition to the dance floor, managing to squeeze 7 grown adults into the photobooth we pass on the way. May surprises us all with an impromptu rendition of Drake's "Nice For What," and clearly, it's a well-practiced routine. The group makes space for her as she raps confidently.

I may not go clubbing often, but I had no idea cheesy dance moves were still so popular. In just one song, I witness Dani pull off a flawless 'fishhook' on Stella from across the room, Anna and May bust out the 'q-tip,' and Sam's robot shuffle to the bar.

The real highlight is watching Anna dance amidst the chaos. She is constantly moving her hips and jumping with unrestrained joy, lighting up the room whenever her favourite songs play – which seemed to be all of them. I find myself drawn to her, unable to resist dancing nearby, longing for her to dance with me. But each time I instinctively reach out to wrap my arms around her, she seems to glide away toward May and Dani.

I'm not a good enough dancer to keep up, despite the drinks fuelling my moves.

A few hours in, Anna waves to the group, shouting over

the music, "It's too hot in here, I'm going to grab some water before I pass out!". With a smile she darts off between the crowded floor towards the bar on the other side of the club.

After a pause, I follow her. I could also do with a drink. I need to hydrate in this hot space. For my health of course.

Making it out of the crowd, I see her at the end of the bar. Watching her leaning over the counter is an unbelievable tease. I feel like a teenager the way my mind goes haywire. I would love to spin her round and put her on the bar to face me. Recreate the night in Cambridge – but go further and longer and harder. Bend her over the bar and tie her arms behind her back with my belt.

Or pick her up and press her against the wall. Hold her hands above her head and kiss her neck until she's begging for more. Preferably somewhere completely empty. But right now, I don't care if a whole crowd lines up behind us to watch.

Feeling the drinks giving me a healthy dose of Dutch courage, I step up close behind Anna, putting my hands either side of her on the bar, trying to ignore the images running wild in my head.

She jumps in alarm and turns to see me, spinning between my arms holding her in place. Her look of alarm doesn't completely disappear, but she smiles up at me in amusement. Being with her in my flat is one thing but seeing her out with her friends brimming with confidence, dancing and laughing like this, it's driving me wild.

"Needed a break from dancing?" she shouts over the noise, leaning her elbows back on the bar to better look up at me.

"Something like that," I shout back. The way she's arching her back, her hair falling over her shoulders to show her collarbone, it's like an invitation to bite her neck.

I lean in closer, moving towards her to speak softly. Her lips part slightly as her eyes dart across my face. I'm so close now my lips brush her ear as I say, "Or maybe I just wanted to see you."

Her skin seems to tingle against mine, and I can feel her shoulders shudder ever so slightly as my stubble brushes her cheek.

Her face turns as I start to move back, so our noses touch. I can't tell if it's the music, or my heart beating against my chest, as her face moves up to mine ever so slowly. Holding the breath of space between our lips feels like a heavenly torture.

After holding the moment for another breath, I can't resist and move down to kiss her. Her face tilts up towards me as we intertwine. I thread my arms around her waist, and her hands move between us just above my jeans, pulling against my t-shirt in desperation to bring me closer.

The kiss becomes deeper and more passionate. She presses her body flush against me, so I put my hands on her hips and push her firmly back against the bar. I love how I can feel her straining against me, as if still wanting more despite how completely wrapped up we already are. Her hands brush against the skin under my t-shirt, sending shivers through me and making me smile even as we kiss. It's almost intoxicating how much I can tell she wants this too.

I bring one hand up to her hair and pull her face back

from mine. She looks completely undone, just as she did when I first went down on her. That image is now running wild in my head and I'm struggling to think of anything else. Remembering her thighs under my hands, leaving bruises where no one else would see them.

And yet it's even better the way she looks right now. The way her pupils are completely dark. The way she's practically gasping for air. The way her cheeks are flushed.

I can feel the eyes of the people around us, but they all just blur into the background. I'm about to move in to kiss her again when someone bumps into me hard, forcing me to let go of Anna to avoid accidentally pulling her hair. Good when planned, bad when not.

May's standing behind us with two empty cups in hand, looking cheerfully oblivious to what she interrupted by stumbling in.

"Sorry! In need of water!" she yells with a smile.

I look back at Anna, who's still breathing heavily. She grabs the glasses and turns back to the bar.

I turn away to hide my smile, feeling extremely happy about what's happening. Rubbing the back of my neck to try and focus elsewhere I stand and wait. If May can head back to the dance floor, Anna and I can pick up where we left off.

Anna picks up the two filled cups of water from the bar and passes one to May while taking a big swig of the other. Just looking at her makes me want to pull her against me and tease her until she can barely breathe.

She turns to me, offering me the rest of her water. I can't quite read her expression, something else from the lustful look she had before. Taking the water with thanks, she smiles at me.

"Ready to return to the dance floor?" she asks.

No – let's go find a dark corner and get my hands under your shirt. I want you to sit on top of me so I can kiss your neck and bite your ear until you take me home. I want you so badly I don't know how else to show you, is what I wanted to say. Instead, I say, "Sure" and put on a smile to follow her and May back.

For whatever reason – Anna must not want to do the same. Taking the hint, I try to maintain a bit of distance for the rest of the night. Thankfully we don't stay much longer, because I'm torn between wanting to go and keep thinking about that kiss by myself or getting annoyed that we were cut off.

When the time comes to leave, she hugs me goodbye. I have to let go quickly, or I'll struggle to release her at all. As Anna walks away with May, she glances back, her smile lighting up my night. I stare after her, lost in the moment, until Leo punches me in the chest, asking which bus I'm taking.

Chapter 21. Her.

It's hard to believe that Ryan and I have been 'friends with benefits' or whatever you want to call it for almost two months now, and honestly, it's been nothing short of incredible. The chemistry between us is electric, but what really stands out is how everything else seems to melt away the moment I see him. All my stress and worries dissipate, as if I'm stepping into my own personal oasis. It's an unfamiliar feeling, and I can't quite pinpoint why it feels this way.

Maybe it's the comfort of keeping things casual – I don't have to worry about how he feels or what he thinks of me. But then again, maybe there's just something special about Ryan.

It's like nothing I've ever felt before. The strangest evidence of this is every time we spend the night together, I fall right asleep. The first time I stayed over, I was shocked to wake up after a solid eight hours, completely unaware of when I'd dozed off. Honestly, I probably wouldn't have stayed if I'd been thinking clearly, but I felt so comfortable and relaxed, I couldn't resist.

Since then, I've woken up in his arms every time, and while it's a bit embarrassing, it feels incredible. It's like dozing off in a sunlit park, waking up surrounded by warmth and feeling completely at ease.

We've been seeing each other most weeks since, always at his place. When he came over for cocktails, it felt comfortingly familiar at the flat, but that makes it harder to draw a line around our time together. I need to keep him separate from my everyday life, or I might start getting too attached and thinking about us as something more than we are.

The kiss at the club was unexpected. Hot and incredible. But unexpected. I should have guessed something like that would have happened, but I guess I didn't think it would come from Ryan. I desperately wanted his hands on me all night, but I was fighting to keep my distance. I wasn't expecting him to move in like that.

I was kind of glad when May interrupted us, it stopped me melting into him completely. If he had come home after that it would have become something different. It would have pulled whatever it is we're doing into the real world.

I still haven't told Dani about Ryan. I'm not sure how to bring it up, and I worry that talking about it might make me think or feel things I can't – like how much I like him, how great he is, and how I could listen to him talk about his favourite paintings, books, and wines all day long.

How he feels like home.

So far, I've managed to keep those feelings in check.

With the wedding only a few months away, Dani and Leo are in full planning mode, so we haven't had any big group hang outs since our Ballie Ballerson night. Which conveniently makes it easier to keep Ryan separate, not thinking about how nicely he could fit into my friends and life.

Right now, I'm in a very happy place to keep me distracted – a cake shop with Dani on a Saturday afternoon. It's early January, and because the universe didn't think that they were busy enough right now, Leo had a great opportunity pop up last week. He works in fund management in the city, something fancy and financial. Something has come up in a smaller company that focusses on carbon neutral investments, which is perfect for him.

In his absence, I have been tagged into wedding support. Which times itself perfectly with cake tasting in East London.

Although while it should be distracting, as we walk in, I immediately think of Ryan. Damn it.

I can't help it if being surrounded by cakes reminds me of the cheesecake he made last week. As part of his job, he's always looking for new recommendations for clients and restaurants, which means finding the perfect pairings. Desserts is a tricky one (apparently) as not everyone likes dessert wine, so if you're having something sweet after dinner you need something else to recommend.

He baked a cheesecake to do a mini tasting in his flat, which fortunately timed with one of my visits. Just in case he wasn't gorgeous and sexy enough, he can bake. It was incredible. It was like Paul Hollywood himself had stopped by Brixton for the night. And I have a high bar for this, because baked cheesecake is my favourite.

The wine was nice too and complemented beautifully. Ryan seemed particularly happy that evening, so he must have found the perfect match. Something about eating incredible food, and laughing in the kitchen about how well either of us would do on bake off, made for some truly gold standard sex after. Even if I was pretty full of three slices of cheesecake.

Picturing him laughing at the table, coming very close to falling off his chair, while I insist I could make a winning showstopper exclusively out of fondant icing and a can-do attitude, has me smiling to myself as I look at my cake. This is dangerous territory.

I'm meant to be distracting myself from beautiful daydreams of beautiful boys. Back to the cake and friend in front of me. Dani had just been telling me about this event she went to, let's get back to that instead.

"What exactly is a ben-do?" I ask Dani, as we settle into our table.

"It's like a 'hen-do', that has nothing to do with a wedding, but is in fact bento box tasting," Dani says, like this is the most logical thing in the world.

"This isn't your secret hen-do I'm not invited to?" I ask.

"Yes, it is, you're right. Despite saying I don't want a hen-do, and you being my Maid of Honour, I actually just wanted to have a hen-do without you. But still tell you about it afterwards to make you feel bad. This is my way of telling you," Dani says gravely.

"Well, I appreciate your honesty," I say, laughing.

"Slash – it was actually just a work social. Bit of bonding with the colleagues," Dani clarifies.

"Bonding is nice! How is the new team?" I ask enthusiastically. It sounded like Dani had settled in wonderfully to her new job so far. It's always great seeing your friends flourish around you. She continues to inspire me with her courage to try new things and put herself out there in new ways, while I'm too afraid to leave the job I can barely face week on week.

"It's nice! Everyone is so friendly, and I love that they do fun events like this. It's cool how settled I feel in such a short time, I'm already mentoring new people which is wild as I was the new one so recently. I guess it's easy because I know what the newbies need to know," she says, as our cake tasters start to arrive.

"Or, because you're doing an amazing job already, they know you can lead and coach those around you?" I say defiantly. "They wouldn't ask you to mentor someone unless they thought you were going to do a great job. They have no incentive for poor performance."

Dani smiles at me over the spread of cakes. "Thanks Anna. It is nice feeling like you're doing a good job. Currently my biggest issue at work is not getting too drunk during socials."

"Which is a difficult task, but I bet you're doing a great job there too," I say, spearing lemon drizzle onto my fork, dropping a chunk of sugar in my lap in the process. "You know people always say wedding planning is so hard, but this is a treat."

"Yeah," says Dani, passing me a napkin, "this is what it's like all the time. Sitting around eating cake. Basically, just living my Marie Antoinette fantasy."

"Hopefully with a better ending," I say, gratefully taking the napkin.

"Maybe, but it could be a dramatic wedding to remember if not?"

I nod in agreement, moving to the red velvet. "In all seriousness, what is left to do? Cake and…"

"Venue is done, invites sent, hall is booked, dress is being altered and apparently Leo's suit is done. So maybe just the cake?" Dani says counting off her fingers.

"I am incredibly impressed with how you've turned this around. This is the magic when two Type A people come together," I say in awe, making Dani smile with thanks.

"Now that the wedding planning is all moving ahead nicely, I can turn my attention back to you. I feel like I've barely seen you the past weeks, which is my bad for being so wedding centric, so please – what's going on with you? Catch me up on Anna," Dani says expectantly, doing a little happy dance as she takes a bite of the particularly decadent chocolate fudge.

"If you can't put yourself first for wedding planning, when can you?" I say, to give myself a minute to think of what to say. Work is crazy and miserably intense as usual, and because of this I haven't been dating anyone. I've been true to my promise of toning down my fuckboy behaviour, so there's only Ryan. Which I'm still not sure about sharing. I don't want to lie to Dani, but I'm not sure if he wants people to know.

Unable to think of anything else, I say, "Nothing major to be honest. Work is crazy, and I've been seeing someone very low key which has been great. I know it can't go anywhere though, so it's just a bit of light relief." One of the lightest, happiest reliefs I've ever found.

Dani looks excited but tries to match my casual tone.

"That sounds like good potential. Why can't it go anywhere? Who are they? How did you meet them? What are they like?" she says, the excitement spilling through her questions.

"They don't want anything serious. They just had a big breakup and have a lot going on, so they wouldn't want an actual relationship," I stop short of saying 'with me' because I know it would prompt Dani into giving a 'you're so great' speech.

Grabbing another forkful of red velvet for emotional support, I continue, "But they're really sweet. Super gorgeous, but also quite shy sometimes? And a massive nerd. It's only when you get them chatting properly they start getting super animated, it's cute." I pause to stop myself from going on.

Looking back up at Dani, she looks like she's still trying to control her excitement. I raise an eyebrow at her, "What?"

"You just seem kind of excited about them. I haven't seen you excited about someone since Jack," she says, which is probably true.

Jack was someone I really liked last year. He asked me out after we met at a friend's 30th and was initially very keen, leading to some fantastic dates. Then he faded and ghosted me.

"Ah yes, happy memories," I say through a mouthful of cake. Some of it was happy, but it was an intense burn bright then fade away, and the fading really hurt. He was fresh out of a big breakup so I should have known better that he wasn't looking for anything serious. Just like Ryan, I guess.

"Well maybe it's worth trying to sniff out if it could be more serious?" Dani asks.

I look up and scrunch up my face in pain, "That sounds terrible."

"High risk, high reward. If you really like them, maybe it's worth it?"

"True. But he's said he doesn't want something serious – so I can't see why that would have changed," I say, feeling something flicker inside as I start to entertain this idea for a second.

"Well, now you've spent more time together, maybe he can see how incredible you are and how lucky he would be to be with you," Dani says sincerely. She is an incredible hype woman.

"Dani, stop flirting with me, you're engaged."

After the cake tasting, I felt amazing. Spending time with Dani and indulging in cake had been a delightful escape. But as soon as I settled into bed that night, the blissful feeling evaporated. The moment my head hit the pillow, a sudden restlessness surged within me. Stress bubbled up like acid, coursing painfully through my veins.

There's something about lying still that traps the feeling in my legs, leaving me twisting and untwisting beneath the duvet, desperate to shake off this restless energy.

Eventually, I force myself out of bed, heading to the kitchen for toast in a futile attempt to distract myself. Standing in the dark, I stare out the window, taking slow, deep breaths. The cool night air brushes against my skin, slightly easing the tension inside.

Back in bed, after a few more hours scrolling through my phone, I finally drift off in the early morning.

I couldn't help but think about Ryan. I wish he were here with me. I pictured him lying beside me, his chest rising and falling in a gentle rhythm, peacefully lost in dreams. Just imagining him brings a flicker of calm, and I close my eyes, longing to move closer, to feel the warmth of his skin against mine.

But as I open my eyes, the fantasy feels bittersweet, knowing I couldn't ask him to come over. I wouldn't expect him to respond so late on Saturday anyway but asking him over just to hold me isn't part of the deal.

Waking up early on Sunday, I finally text Ryan to ask if he's free in the next few days.

Resisting texting Ryan has become a bit of a habit. I have the urge to text him all the time. I want to tell him about a show I started that he might like, or when we had wine tasting in the office, or ask him what his favourite kind of cake is, or just how his day is going.

I'm strictly avoiding texting him at all, unless it's to make plans to sleep together. I'm scared it might slip into friendly conversation, and there's nothing worse than getting attached and waiting for someone's text.

That was what killed me with Jack. His replies could be a bit slow, then one day he left me unanswered for days and it completely consumed me. All I could do was wonder why he wasn't responding to me. Did I say the wrong thing? Did I do something wrong? What had happened?

When he finally replied with a weak apology, I bravely told him he needed to make more effort or stop talking to me. He chose the latter.

Looking at my phone a few hours later, I see Ryan's reply. "I'm free tonight and all next week till Wednesday evening if any of those work?"

The anxious knot in my chest says the sooner the better, but I know I will be a mess this evening as I'm so tired, so I suggest Monday. May is away on holiday with her family this week, which also gives me free rein to work on a Sunday without anyone to remind me it's a bad idea.

I offer to have him come to mine. At least if I feel the same in the middle of the night again, I can escape to the kitchen.

Turning back to my inbox, I feel a little better.

The intention of working Sunday was to get on top of things, but somehow moving everything forward created a fresh wave of things to do. It's like I accidentally triggered a tsunami.

When I arrive at work, I ignore my inbox and dive into meetings, navigating a flurry of friendly faces seeking help or guidance. The morning rush is relentless, and by lunchtime I find myself retreating to the bathroom, pressing my forehead against the cool wall tiles. I close my eyes, trying to ease the overwhelming sensation that my chest is about to explode. It's like I'm trapped screaming against my own body.

By 6pm I am completely drained and yet wired to my limit. Everyone has left, and I sit alone at my desk trying to stop this wave spilling over into the rest of my week.

Suddenly, I notice it's 8pm, and Ryan will be at my flat in an hour. I'm momentarily torn between my desire to cancel so I can curl up in a ball under my desk, and the bad manners of cancelling. The decision is made a split second later knowing he is probably already on his way, so I hurry out to my car to drive home, very conscious of my hands twitching slightly as I walk.

I can feel tension inside me pushing on my skin, threatening to lose control completely. As I drive home, I take one hand off the wheel and slowly open and close it with all the pressure I can, like I'm holding an invisible stress ball. It doesn't help the tension, but at least feeling the muscles move gives me something to focus on.

Sitting in my car in the garage once I get home, I take a few deep breaths to try and calm down, holding tightly onto the wheel. I wish I had longer nails to dig into my arms, or some way to feel something against my skin to distract me from how I feel inside.

I know if I slow down for one more second, I'll start crying, and as it's almost 9 o'clock there's no time to cry. Grabbing my bag, I walk up to my flat in a daze.

The buzzer goes as I enter, so I let Ryan up with a cheerful hello. Game face on, everything is fine. I'm totally fine.

There's a knock at the door and I take a breath, then answer it. Ryan is standing in a big coat and a hat, smiling down at me.

"Welcome, thanks for coming up north," I say, stepping back to let him in.

"No problem," he says, taking off his jacket and looking down at my bag on my shoulder and shoes still on.

"I literally just got through the door so do you mind if we just grab a drink for a second?" I say, putting down my bag and feeling my hands still tensing and twitching slightly. I move my arms behind my back. Need to get that under control first, then everything will be fine.

"Yeah of course," Ryan says, and I turn to lead him into the kitchen.

"What would you like? Water, coke, beer?" I ask.

"Water would be great, thank you," he says, turning to look at the view out the window.

I take a moment to appreciate his tall frame, drawing me in with his quiet strength. An overwhelming urge washes over me, to slip behind him, to wrap my arms around his waist and press my face into his back, breathing in his familiar scent. I want to lose myself in him, to block out the chaos of the world around us.

In that sudden fantasy, I imagine him turning to me, wrapping his arms around me, holding me tight as if shielding me from everything that weighs me down. I want to believe that suddenly, nothing else would matter. That he's here solely for me, just as I want to be there for him. The thought flashes like a match, a fleeting moment where I can pretend that our connection could be something deeper, something more.

Instead, I turn to grab two glasses of water, my heart racing as I focus on keeping my hands steady. As I walk over, I catch Ryan's gaze, and for a moment, everything else fades away.

"This is a really cool view. I didn't really get to see it past all the cocktails last time," he says, turning back to take the glass from me. His eyes hold a comforting warmth that makes me want to melt.

"Thanks," I reply, settling onto the sofa and taking a small sip, my fingers nervously fiddling with my ring. The metal feels cool against my skin, but it does nothing to stop the painful static energy building inside me.

Ryan sits down beside me, his expression curious, almost searching. "Are you okay?"

"Yep, all good. Just need a second to kind of let the day fade away, you know?" I smile as brightly as I can, hoping to deflect his concern. "How was your day?"

He tilts his head, a hint of worry etching his features. "It was fine…Are you sure you're okay?"

His words pierce through the walls that I'm trying to hold up, and the urge to let everything go becomes overwhelming. I feel tears prickling at the corners of my eyes, and I instinctively look away. "Sorry, it's just…work was a bit much today, and I'm feeling a bit…" My voice trails off, a whisper lost in the silence.

Without hesitation, he moves closer, wrapping his arms around me in a gentle embrace. The warmth of his body against mine sends the tears spilling over, and I find myself quietly crying into his chest. I try to apologise, but he shushes me softly, his fingers soothingly running through my hair.

In that moment, everything trapped inside me begins to fade, like a storm giving way to a calm morning light. Being held by him feels like a sanctuary, a safe harbour from the chaos of my thoughts. He shifts slightly, pulling me in more securely, and I tuck my legs beneath me, feeling completely enveloped in Ryan's warmth. It's perfect, almost surreal.

We sit together, wrapped in this comfort, and it takes several deep breaths before I can finally pull away. Ryan reaches for a tissue from the coffee table, his eyes reflecting genuine concern.

"Thanks, and sorry," I say, wiping my eyes, feeling a mixture of embarrassment and gratitude.

"Please don't apologise for getting stressed and upset. I know how much you care about your work. I'm sorry your day has been so awful," he says softly, his arm resting on the back of the sofa, the other casually draped over my leg, still keeping me close even as I pull away.

"It wasn't even a bad day. Nothing bad happened. It was just too long, too intense, and…too much," I admit, feeling the weight of a thousand responsibilities pressing down on me.

"Maybe those things make it a bad day, even if nothing bad happened?" Ryan suggests, his thumb brushing away a stray tear from my cheek.

"Maybe," I murmur, my gaze falling to my hands, which are starting to feel normal again. His fingers linger against my cheek, and I close my eyes, savouring the simple touch that sends a wave of warmth through me. I gently flex my hands in my lap, the tension slowly dissipating.

"Thanks for being so nice about it. I'm fine, honestly. I just needed a moment."

"It's okay if you're not fine," Ryan replies, frowning slightly. "It's not a problem, except for the fact that you're upset, obviously."

"There's just so much to do, and I really hate disappointing people," I confess, looking down at where one of his hands rests on top of mine. The painful electricity inside me seems to melt into something soothing at his touch, the warmth of his skin igniting a longing within me.

"You're not disappointing anyone," Ryan says firmly, his gaze steady. "You can't always be winning and doing everything perfectly. Some days, just being good is good enough."

I take a deep breath, trying to let his words sink in. They resonate so deeply, yet I struggle to fully believe them. His kindness feels so comforting, and I can't help but wonder: is this what a relationship is supposed to feel like?

"Yes, well, thanks. And I'm really sorry, but I'm probably not up for anything tonight. I know you came all the way here, and I really appreciate it. You're welcome to stay over if you want, I know it's late," I say, acutely aware of the inconvenience I've caused. He travelled here, only to have me cry on him. The thought of him leaving fills me with an unexpected dread, but the words to ask him to stay remain stuck in my throat.

"Of course, don't worry about it. If it's okay with you, I'd really like to stay," Ryan replies, a warm smile spreading across his face. My heart lifts as I nod enthusiastically, feeling the knot in my chest begin to unravel. His presence is so calming, and even amidst my tears, I feel a sense of relief.

"Maybe we can watch a movie or something?" Ryan suggests, glancing toward the big screen opposite us. "I mean, if you want?"

"That sounds great," I say, surprised at how perfect that actually sounds. As I feel more like myself, the idea of a little escapism and comfort feels like just what I need to complete this healing process. "If you still haven't seen *Dredd*, let's watch that."

"From what you've said, I definitely want to, but do you want something lighter?" he asks, looking slightly confused.

"*Dredd* is light – just in a violent, futuristic, drug-bust kind of way," I reply, grabbing the remote. "The only thing is it's quite long, so we can only start it if you're okay with stopping halfway through." He agrees, and my heart swells at the thought of watching this film with him. It feels like an incredible treat that I don't quite believe I deserve.

"Hold on a sec, I need to change into leggings," I say, feeling calmer now, the weight of the evening lifting. When I return, I find Ryan lounging comfortably, feet up, his arm draped casually along the back of the sofa, gesturing for me to join him at his side. Whether he's extending comfort to help me stop crying or simply wants me there doesn't matter

– I nestle in, treasuring every point of contact between us as I click play.

"Thank you," I whisper, glancing up at him, my heart racing.

"You're welcome," he replies, his voice soft and sincere. Then, he leans down to kiss my forehead, and the gesture sends a shiver of warmth cascading through me. As Karl Urban appears on screen, I can't help but think how incredibly lucky I am to have Ryan beside me.

Sitting together we feel like two puzzle pieces interlocked, but softer. Like two leaves fallen from the same tree, lying side by side on the grass.

In this moment, wrapped in his presence, I feel a flicker of hope that maybe, just maybe, what we have is something truly special.

Chapter 22. Him.

Monday night was amazing. I mean it was terrible seeing Anna like that. I can't believe the pressure she puts on herself, or that others put on her. It can be hard to tell which way it is. But being there for her was amazing. It felt like Anna really opened up and let me in, which is a first.

The rest of our Monday felt really special and comfortable. We watched the first half of *Dredd*, she was right, it's an incredible movie, or a 'sick film' as she would say. We then went to bed where she embraced being close together straight away. Normally she keeps her distance and it's only once she's asleep or dozing off that she finds her way into my arms or pressed up against my back like a tiny spoon. Maybe it was the time together on the sofa, where we were so close emotionally, that made her lean into the physical closeness as well. I don't know, but I loved it. She always has to get up crazy early for work (6:30 wake for a 7am drive feels crazy to me at least) so we didn't chat much in the morning, but I gave her a big hug before I left. She looked much calmer than the night before, so I hoped she was feeling better inside as well.

The early start worked well because I had to head to the airport for 9am anyway to catch a flight. I had a last minute invite for a wine conference in Italy for the next few days. I realised on the way out that I didn't get a chance to tell Anna about it as we had avoided work topics for the rest of the evening, basking in the awe of *Dredd*.

Heading to the airport on the tube I have a moment to reflect on how much more comfortable I am in London than before. I feel like the past couple of months I have really started to settle into London life. Sam and Dani have been so welcoming, and I've joined their Saturday morning 'bouldering & coffee' routine when I'm not working. I've made some friends at work (not Tom to be clear) like Garett who works in the shop and who has a remarkable tie collection. He lives in South Clapham with his family and makes for excellent wine tasting company. Some of the guys in the office have also started inviting me for regular after work drinks.

I've started to get the tube, knowing which lines go where and I now know how to get to certain parts of the city. I even helped someone with directions last week, which felt like a huge achievement. It feels like I've really made my life here in London my own. Like this is where I belong.

After a gruelling journey filled with crying children and one ironically anxious support animal, I finally meet my colleagues in Rome. The talks at the conference are fantastic, and the wine is predictably superb. I'm kept busy all day networking with potential clients until late in the evening. When I finally make it to my room and collapse into bed, I check my phone and see a text from Anna: "Thank you again for last night, it meant a lot. It would be really nice to see you again this week if you're keen? Just let me know when works :)."

I smile to myself as I read it again. It feels warmer than her usual scheduling messages, more personal. She doesn't typically text so soon after seeing me. Is this a hint at something deeper? "Really nice to see you again" feels like a big step up from her usual "Are you around this week?"

I lean back in bed, trying to think it through. My mind is too tired to make sense of it right now. The idea of moving beyond casual with Anna is exciting, but what does she mean? Is this romantic, or is she just being friendly? Am I reading too much into it, or is it genuinely a shift?

Considering if it is romantic, my heart starts to race. Am I ready for that? I feel like I'm starting to put down roots in London, so maybe I am ready for something more serious. But this is a lot to decode at midnight. With the next few days in Italy looming, I decide it's best to reply tomorrow when I'm less exhausted and can craft the right response. As I'm away anyway it doesn't make any difference if I wait to reply once I have more time, and I don't want to risk changing our dynamic if I'm not sure if I'm ready for it. As I set my phone down to sleep, I can't help but smile to myself, feeling a lot happier than before.

Unfortunately, the next few days are a whirlwind, leaving little room for contemplation. Networking is crucial for my job, but it's exhausting to stay on my game all day. Anna's text lingers in the back of my mind as I return to my room the following night. I'm caught in a tug-of-war between asking her out on a date and keeping things casual. What if I suggest a date and she says no, effectively ending things altogether? I don't want to rush this decision and risk making a mistake.

Plus, the wine community loves to drink, so there are a lot of small tastings that stretch late into the evening, leaving me a little tipsy every night. It's not until the conference wraps up on Friday that I finally have a moment to myself, away from the crowds and glasses of wine. Sitting in the airport, I pull up Anna's text again.

Seeing her message makes me feel hopeful. This could be a sign. As I wait for my gate, I reach a conclusion: I want to date her properly. I don't want to keep it casual anymore, but it feels like something we should discuss in person. The next time I see her, I want to sit down and talk, maybe even stop her from running away or distracting me with kisses.

I'm not the most articulate over text, so I think face-to-face is my best shot. I type out a reply: "Sorry for the slow response! My absolute pleasure. I'd love to do something soon, are you free this weekend? Saturday night?" Hitting send, I know it's late notice, but I hope there's a gap in her schedule.

Feeling satisfied with my message, I put my music back on and try to relax for the journey home.

Sitting in a coffee shop with Leo on Saturday morning, I still haven't had a reply from Anna. Ignoring the anomaly of my unusually slow texting this week, we normally have relatively swift responses. Both of our jobs keep us off our phones during the day. But in the evenings or at the weekends, it's normally pretty quick. I put my phone away, hoping she's not gotten lost in a new mess of work.

Leo raises an eyebrow at me, his expression a mix of curiosity and concern. "What's on your phone?"

"What do you mean?" I feign innocence, trying to act casual.

"You keep glancing at it. Are you bidding on eBay or something?"

I let out a sigh and take a sip of my coffee, another of Leo's spot-on recommendations. It's delicious, but it's not enough to distract me. "No, just waiting on a text to nail down some plans."

"Ah, okay." He takes a sip, his knowing smile growing. "Is it maybe a girl? Who's keeping you waiting?"

"Maybe," I say, my annoyance bubbling just beneath the surface.

Leo leans back, clearly enjoying the moment. "You know, the silence isn't going to make me stop guessing."

I hesitate. I haven't told him about Anna yet, but with my feelings growing stronger, maybe now is the time to share and get his advice. If only he can tone down that smugness. "I've sort of been seeing someone," I say, watching for his reaction. Leo's face stays blank. "Actually, it's someone you know."

Still nothing.

"It's Anna."

He nods slowly, as if confirming a hypothesis. "We thought so."

"We?"

"Me and Dani. Also, Sam and Stella, but for them, it was more of a conspiracy theory. Mine was closer to scientific fact."

"Well, your 'facts' were right. We haven't been dating properly; it's been...casual." I can't help the defensiveness creeping in.

"Seems like it's going really well," he says, raising an eyebrow, clearly sceptical.

"It was going okay, but I feel like we're on the brink of something more. I'm finally settled in here, and it feels like we're getting...closer? If that makes sense." I'm not used to opening up about relationships, but this feels worth the risk. Especially since it's my best friend's fiancée's best friend we're talking about. The social ramifications could be endless, and I really don't want to stir up any drama.

Leo takes it surprisingly well, looking relaxed instead of shocked. "Well, you said it yourself. Anna's great. You two would be a solid match, so you have my blessing."

"Not that I was looking for it," I add quickly, but I can't help feeling a weight lift off my shoulders. "And you really think I should go for it?"

"Absolutely." He sets his coffee down, looking serious.

"But do you think she would want to?" I can't help but ask. The distance she keeps makes me doubt her feelings, even if our moments together are electric.

"Can't see why not," he replies, though it's not the most reassuring answer. "And if she doesn't, Anna's cool. She won't be rude about it, she'll just tell you. I wouldn't worry about awkwardness, just go for it. Worst-case scenario? She says no."

That's a pretty big worst-case for me. "What if I ruin your wedding with all the drama? It's only a couple of months away!" I shoot back, trying to maintain my most serious expression.

Leo just laughs, completely unfazed.

By Sunday evening when I still haven't heard from Anna, I start to get worried. I'm sure if something had happened she would have told Dani, who would have told Leo, who would have told me. But what if she's just stuck in her room getting overwhelmed with work unable to take a step out?

I wonder for a second if I should go over, but that might be a bit intense. I remember her saying on Monday she didn't have any big weekend plans which is why the late reply is so concerning, but maybe something came up last minute and she's actually just having a good weekend and not looking at her phone.

Still, I send her another message, "Hey, just wanted to check if you're alright? No worries about the weekend, I know it was last minute. But I hope that work isn't too much at the moment. Let me know when may work."

A few minutes later my phone buzzes with a text from Anna. Great. Opening it up I see, "Hey sorry for not replying it's been busy. It's been really great hanging out with you, but

I don't think we should continue anymore. I definitely still want to be friends if that's okay? Have a great evening :) Xx."

Well, fuck.

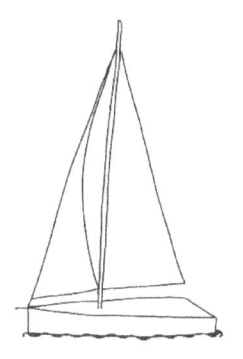

Chapter 23. Her.

I stare at the point over the edge of the bed where my phone has just fallen off, having thrown it there a few seconds ago.

After a moment of silence, May turns to me slowly, "Do you want me to go and see if he's replied?"

"Yes please," I say in a quiet voice.

May has been hearing updates all week – or rather, the lack of them.

It all started with the initial excitement of Monday night, although "excitement" feels like a generous term. I ended up in tears as I recounted the evening to her. It wasn't about work, it was the stress of being so vulnerable with Ryan.

My ex-boyfriend saw me crying as an annoyance, something that always managed to create a problem for him. And somehow, I was always left apologising for it. My favourite incident was when he was angry the day after I cried at a party because it was so embarrassing for him.

With that in mind, I found it frightening to think about crying in front of Ryan. He had made me feel comfortable in the moment, but once he left, I couldn't shake the nagging worry about what he might have thought.

On my drive to work the next morning, I called May for her perspective. She believed Ryan genuinely liked me and wanted something more than just a casual thing. I could see the logic in her reasoning, but it felt hard to believe. My romantic judgment has been questionable in the past, so I decided to trust May's judgement instead.

When I arrived at work, I texted Ryan to thank him and suggested going out again. My plan was to propose a dinner or a drink, something more substantial than a late night flat visit.

When he didn't reply after a day, I told myself he might be busy. After two days, I began to worry, he usually responded the same day or by the next morning. By Thursday evening, hope faded.

May had plans that night, leaving me home alone, binge-eating and watching *Pirates of the Caribbean*. It was a shame because I usually love that movie. Ryan also may have completely ruined *Dredd* for me.

It was Jack all over again. When things start to feel too good to be true, they often are. I should have realized that Ryan was just being polite, being a good friend, but not looking for anything deeper. It's been said before, but this silence is deafening.

That night, I went to bed early and archived his messages,

hoping that if he did reach out again, at least it wouldn't ruin my day. I had every intention of being polite and friendly, regardless of the ghosting, when I saw his message on Friday afternoon.

The familiar sting of a late reply hit me hard. I can't endure this again, it's emotionally and physically draining. I can't invest in someone who isn't interested – and I shouldn't. I'm trying to stop myself from falling for people who won't put in the effort. Just because he's a nice guy who will comfort you when you're upset, doesn't mean he wants to date you.

I held off replying out of sheer exhaustion. Ironically, after my evening with Ryan, my work had improved that week. I managed to set some reasonable boundaries, taking actual lunch breaks and not working past 7pm. Baby steps, but impactful ones. Still, the week was tiring, and the emotional weight of waiting after being so vulnerable on Monday felt unbearable.

On Sunday, May and I sat in my room, debating how to respond to Ryan's slow Friday reply. I can't ghost him, that feels cowardly. But I also don't know how to politely end things. The emotional toll of the week has completely overshadowed the joy he brought me. If he found Monday overwhelming and this subtle ghosting is his way of signalling he wants to keep it casual, I won't try to convince him otherwise.

We're almost done with the draft when he texts asking if I'm okay, almost giving me a heart attack. Ironic that he's asking if I'm okay for not replying after his slow reply? Unbelievable.

I hit send and throw my phone. May dutifully and lovingly fetches it, and we look at the screen.

Ryan is typing. Why do people go cliff diving for adrenaline, they can just watch their crush text rejections instead.

Ryan stops typing. Ryan is offline.

"Okay, well that's that." I say. Putting my phone down next to me in a calmer way.

"I'm sorry it didn't work out," May says kindly, "but well done for knowing what you need and protecting yourself. I know it's been hard this week."

"Thanks hun," I say, lying back on the bed. At least it's over, no more turmoil or questions, I can just move on. At least for the next month or so before I see him at the wedding.

The first few weeks after everything ended flew by. Taking Ryan's advice to just be good enough and finally recognising the cost of overworking did wonders for me.

And sometimes, even if you're fighting hard to do a job well, that doesn't mean you should. Maybe it's just the wrong role for you – especially when the alternative is coming home in tears.

It took some time, but I started setting real boundaries, giving myself the headspace I desperately needed. Eventually, I realised the problem wasn't just that the job was hard. It wasn't the right fit. The ways of working, the constant firefighting – I have been trying to prove to myself that I can do this and excel here, but I just didn't enjoy it. It didn't suit me, and if I'm being completely honest it drained me.

As someone who's always stepped up and thrown myself into whatever challenge came my way, coming to that realisation was incredibly hard. I'd been pouring everything I had into trying to bring my most enthusiastic, passionate self to work – and it was killing me.

When I finally spoke to my manager, it took some time for her to really hear me. There was a bit of misleading optimism on her part – trying to convince me I could still do what I love in the same role – but eventually, I was clear, I needed to move.

Thankfully, despite the relentless misery of the past year, I'd maintained a solid reputation and strong network. So, when I made the decision, finding a new opportunity didn't take long. In three weeks, I'm moving back into the Strategy team – and I honestly can't wait.

I've already started picking up a few projects as part of my handover, and it's wild how different it feels. This is the kind of work I love – challenging, fast-paced, but in a way that feels joyful and thrilling, not painful.

Since stepping away from Operations, I can finally see how tough things really were. Turns out it's not normal to end the day with a burning desire to throw your laptop at a colleague.

Workdays are starting to feel enjoyable again. Without the constant high-stakes drama, I'm rediscovering the parts of work I actually like – building friendships, joining extracurriculars, all the things I've neglected in the chaos.

Accepting that "good enough" really is enough is still a work in progress. But I'm getting there. And it's already easier to flourish in a space where I feel strong and capable, instead of one where I have to fight tooth and nail just to stay afloat.

This shift has created so much more mental space and joy for other activities, like seeing friends and going horse riding. In the past, every encounter with a friend felt overshadowed by a dark cloud of stress and fatigue. Now, I feel more like myself, able to relax on weekends and engage in activities for fun, rather than as a means to hold off a breakdown. Going for a ride now is a real treat, knowing I won't have any missed calls from work waiting for me.

I'm getting back into a solid routine, spending my weekends exercising and meal prepping instead of working. While some work stress still lingers, a hot bath and a friendly conversation are often enough to put the stress at bay and help me sleep soundly.

All of my friends have tried to land this message with me before, but I really have Ryan to thank for getting it across to me. He saw a side of me I always try to keep hidden, and somehow, with him, I found myself opening up in ways I never knew I could.

The downside of this newfound healthy work-life balance is that I now have more mental space for other things, like missing Ryan.

I had hoped I wouldn't. I've trained myself to let go of romantic relationships, and I associated him with a necessary escape from work. As the stress faded, I thought maybe I could move on without him. But this new sense of calm has only deepened my longing for him.

Now, I see the positive impact he had on my life, and I

have more time to reflect on just how wonderful he is – cute, sweet, and funny. I think about how much he loves Leo, *Lord of the Rings*, and his job – which only makes him more attractive to me. And that's no small feat, considering how handsome he is.

He did eventually reply to my text a couple of days later saying "Of course, no problem. Let's be friends." I haven't seen him since that teary Monday. I think Dani and Leo may be coordinating us as passing ships in the night, in between all the wedding planning.

Ryan may be able to miss lunch with friends to avoid me, but I have a feeling as the Best Man he'll be turning up to this one.

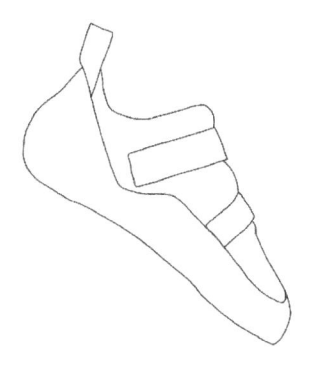

Chapter 24. Him.

Watching Nicki nurse her forearms, I can't help but feel a slight, smug sense of satisfaction. It's my turn to drag my flatmate into a random early morning exercise activity, and oh, how the tables have turned.

"I thought you were supposed to be in good shape?" I can't resist teasing, letting out a small laugh.

Nicki looks up at me, unimpressed, from where she's sitting on the mats.

"This is a ridiculous activity. When in the Harrison Ford am I ever going to need to climb a giant rock?" she grumbles, as I sit down next to her.

"Unlike Reformer Pilates, which is apparently essential to survival. I just can't get through a day at work without someone tying up my ankles," I say with a grin.

"I didn't realise wine-buying was such a spicy crowd," Sam

shouts across to us, where he's standing a few meters away, watching Dani tackle a particularly challenging route. Normally, my height gives me an advantage in sports, but watching Dani spider-monkey her way around the holds – hanging upside down, leaping from one spot to another – makes me think she has the upper hand here.

We're at the Mile End Climbing Centre, enjoying the quiet before the rush. These places have the same vibe as a good coffee shop – soft chatter and gentle background music. Thanks to the "Bouldering Babes" WhatsApp group with Dani and Sam, this has become one of my weekly highlights.

Ever since Anna's message, I've been trying my best to accept things and move on, but it's not been easy. I keep replaying the time we spent together in my head, wondering how she's doing now. I haven't seen her since that night at her place, and it's killing me.

Spending time with Dani and Sam is fun though. It's been great getting closer to them, and it helps take my mind off things.

Bringing Nicki along is partly about doing the same for her. She's been really down lately, spending most of her time holed up in the flat which has been worrying.

"We're going to try the other side – are you guys coming?" Sam calls out as Dani drops down from her route, having completed it flawlessly.

Nicki shoots me a slightly panicked look, and I laugh before saying, "I think we'll sit this one out for a bit. We'll catch up with you."

Dani gives us a salute of approval as she and Sam walk

over to the next wall.

"Thanks for dragging me along. Despite the battle wounds, this is actually fun," Nicki says, offering me a smile.

"No problem," I reply, smiling back. I've been holding back from asking her what's really going on, since she keeps insisting nothing's wrong – she's "just a bit tired." But maybe this change of scenery is just what she needs to open up about whatever's weighing on her.

"How's your week been?" I ask innocently.

Nicki gives me an amused frown. "You've seen me almost every day this week, and we spent last night watching *She's the Man* together. You literally know my week as well as I do."

"Okay, I'll be less subtle – how are you?" I say, leaning in slightly.

"I'm fine," she replies calmly, without missing a beat.

I fix her with my friendliest but most assertive expression – the kind I've perfected after years of negotiating at work. "I'm no expert, but I'd say...maybe you're not."

Nicki glances away to watch the climbers, her gaze distant as she seems to weigh her words. I'm aware, as I wait for her response, that I might be being a bit hypocritical. After all, while she's been quietly sulking in the flat, I've been right there beside her, avoiding my own feelings. Who am I to call her out on her misery when I've been bottling up my own?

But nothing changes if nothing changes. "Alex and I are having some issues," she says quietly, breaking the silence between us. "We've been planning to move to Cheshire for the past year, but the more I think about it, the less sure I am that it's actually what I want. I tried talking to him about it a couple of months ago, and he completely shut down. He acted like I was trying to break up with him, just because I wasn't sure about the move. Since then, it's been impossible to talk to him about it."

"That's awful. I'm sorry," I say, gently placing a hand on her arm in support. Nicki looks up at me, and I can see the beginnings of tears welling in her eyes. "I can't know what it's like in your relationship, but I do think you should move somewhere that works for both of you."

"But maybe he's right," Nicki murmurs, wiping the corner of her eye with the back of her hand. "I agreed to move, and now, changing my mind...I feel like I'm asking a lot from him. He'd have to leave his family, his whole life."

"I mean," I say, choosing my words carefully, "he's asking a lot from you too."

Nicki tilts her head, considering. I know how hard it is to confront your partner like this – especially when it feels like you're calling them out on something they don't even see as a problem. I could only get angry with Karina after the breakup. At the time, I just wanted to fix everything, to make it work, to stay with her.

I turn and grab tissues and water from my bag, passing them to her. The climbing wall feels like a safe space for tears, but a drink of water might help turn the occasional tear into something less overwhelming.

"Maybe try talking to him again?" I suggest gently.

"Maybe. But the way he reacted – it was like he couldn't even comprehend what I was saying. Like he didn't get why I might not want to move there. And it just made me wonder...what does he think of me?" Nicki looks at me, her expression calm but puzzled.

"How do you mean?"

"I told him about all the things I'd miss – my work, my friends, the stuff that matters to me – and it was like he just...didn't get it? He just said, 'If this is such an issue, why didn't you say something when we agreed to move in the first place?'" she says, a mix of frustration and hurt in her voice.

"I guess if he doesn't realise how important these things are to you, maybe the key is making sure he does – so he can understand where you're coming from," I offer, though I can tell it's not a perfect solution.

"But that's the thing," she says, her voice a little sharper now, "we've been together for two years. If he doesn't understand me by now – if he doesn't get these huge pieces of my life – then what are we doing?"

I agree. Given how much time Alex and Nicki have spent together, his lack of understanding of her is downright bizarre. It only took me a few weeks to pick up on the key drivers in her life – the things that really light her up. Her energy is contagious when she's meeting new people or getting involved in things around London. How he hasn't noticed that is beyond me.

Telling someone their partner doesn't seem to show enough interest in them is never easy. I consider how best to respond as the soft music plays in the background, drifting through the air like a gentle hum.

"So, what do you think you're going to do?" I ask, keeping my tone casual.

Nicki sits up a little straighter, a small smile playing on her lips. "I have no idea. But I guess stopping the moping around would be a good first step. That includes you, by the way."

"Me?" I blink, taken aback.

She raises an eyebrow, clearly unimpressed. "Don't pretend you haven't been moping right alongside me these past few weeks."

Once again – flatmates are supposed to be cold, distant strangers. While my care for Nicki comes from a good place, I'd really prefer it if she didn't make me confront my own feelings right now.

"I've just been trying to keep you company," I say, trying to deflect.

"Sure. It has nothing to do with a certain someone who hasn't exactly been around lately?" she suggests, with a knowing look.

"It might have something to do with it," I admit, begrudgingly.

"What happened between you two? It seemed like things were going well, for a 'casual' thing anyway," she asks, curious.

I lean back on my arms and look up at the ceiling, as if I might find the answer written there. "I honestly don't know. It seemed like it was going somewhere, and then...it wasn't."

I glance back at Nicki, who's looking at me with an expression of sympathy.

"I'm sorry," she says quietly.

I smile at her. "Thanks."

"No more moping, then?" she says, holding out her hand with a teasing glint in her eyes.

I grin and take it, shaking firmly. "Agreed."

"I thought I was the one meant to be panicking today," Leo says, a smile on his face.

I look up from staring at the floor. Leo's in his new green suit, looking incredibly handsome and radiant. The big day is finally here, and he's the perfect groom. We're sitting just the two of us in one of the Cambridge University buildings, surrounded by wedding decorations.

"That's just something out of terrible, misogynistic movies," I reply.

"What a fun thought for my special day," he chuckles, moving to sit beside me.

"Sorry, I'm just really nervous about seeing Anna. I'm trying not to think about it because it's your day, and you look amazing. I'll probably cry when Dani walks down the aisle, and I'm sure it'll be fine once the ceremony starts, but I can't help it…" I rush out in one breath, my anxiety spilling over.

I shake my head, attempting to dispel my nerves, and give an unconvincing smile. "You look great," I say again, eager to shift the conversation back to him.

"I know," he replies, the self-assured king as always. "But I can't have you moping on my wedding day. If you're feeling this way again, why don't you just commit and ask her out?"

"She's already made it clear she doesn't want to date me," I say, repeating the mantra I've told myself to let it go. Then, processing his words, I add, "What do you mean 'again'?"

"Did she? I thought she just didn't want something casual anymore. That's what she told Dani. I figured you hadn't asked her out because you'd changed your mind about dating." Leo says.

"Wait, what do you mean she 'didn't want something casual'? She said she wanted to stop seeing me," I respond, trying to make sense of his laid-back take.

He looks surprised. "Yeah, but not because she doesn't like you."

"Then why did she end it?" My confusion deepens as I recall the message I've been obsessing over: 'I don't think we should continue anymore.'

"Because she likes you? At least, that's what Dani said." Leo looks genuinely concerned at my inability to understand him. "I don't really get whatever 'casual' arrangement you suggested, but it sounded like she wanted a relationship, and you didn't."

I stare at the carpet, trying to digest this new perspective. Leo continues, "I was surprised when Dani told me it had ended after what you said at the café. I thought maybe you changed your mind or still weren't ready to date."

"If she felt that way, why didn't she just say she wanted to start something serious?" I stand up, rubbing the back of my neck in frustration as I begin to pace.

"I'm no expert, but from what I heard through the grapevine, you mentioned keeping it casual. So, I can see why she might feel hesitant, it would go against everything you've said. And you've heard it, she's had some bad experiences. I don't think she was looking for a challenge – trying to date someone who didn't want to date," Leo explains, watching me pace while he remains unnervingly calm.

He stands and walks over, halting me in my tracks. "Dude, I've known you for years, and I've never seen you look this confused."

"I am," I admit, the weight of it all settling over me. "I'm upset. It's a huge realization – after all these years, you're actually smarter than me." I force a smile, though it feels a little off.

"Glad you're finally catching up." He grins, reaching over to straighten my collar, which had gotten bent out of shape in my distress. "Not to make this all about me, but you might want to pause your train of thought for the next thirty minutes. I may be smarter than you, but I could really use your help getting through the next part of this without looking like an idiot in front of two hundred people."

I look him dead in the eye, trying to suppress a smile. With one hand on his shoulder, I offer a reassuring look. "Don't worry. There's only about a 30% chance you'll fall over."

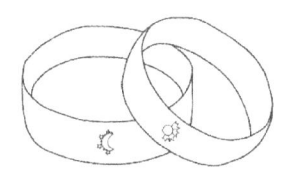

Chapter 25. Her.

It's funny, watching your best friends grow up. It's like watching a sunrise – you're there the whole time, and somehow, you still miss it. Then, all at once, it's a beautiful morning, and you're laughing with someone you love.

Watching Dani laugh with her mum, it's like basking in golden sunlight. Her joy is so bright, I feel like I'm glowing from the inside, the warmth kissing my cheeks.

We're in the unofficial bridal suite, putting the finishing touches to everything before the big moment. I step closer to Dani as Stella and Sandra (Dani's mum) move to unpack the veil. We're all in shades of blue, complimenting Leo's choice of greens. It looks particularly perfect in the bridal suite with its light blue walls and soft white chairs.

"How are you feeling?" I ask softly, standing next to her in the mirror.

She grins at me in the reflection, looking absolutely

stunning in her long silk white dress. "Pretty good." Her smile is the calm confidence of knowing she's making the right decision. And then, of course, here come the tears again.

Dani laughs as she turns to face me. "The ceremony hasn't even started! How are you going to manage once the vows begin?"

"Oh, I won't. Get ready for a puddle on the floor. A new water feature – formerly known as Anna." I joke, trying to hold back the tears threatening to ruin my dress.

"Well, Leo was trying to find ways to make the wedding unique, but I'd rather you keep it together long enough to get to the cake," Dani teases, handing me a tissue.

"I will be fine! Nothing to worry about!"

I'm incredibly worried.

I'm usually a quiet, peaceful crier, but this is a special occasion, and the odds of me becoming a blubbering mess are high. I see puffy eyes and a drippy nose in my future, which is particularly problematic because I know Ryan is somewhere nearby. I mean honestly, it doesn't matter – he's seen me naked, in my pyjamas, drunk on a night out, in the shower, and crying. Still, I hope he thinks I look mind-blowingly beautiful today.

I've been avoiding mentioning him, and Dani's been kind enough to do the same. It's impressive, considering how much of the wedding planning I know Ryan was involved in, yet his name hasn't come up once.

Today is about Dani and Leo – not about how gorgeous I expect Ryan to look in a suit.

"It's almost time, ladies!" Stella announces, pulling me

out of my thoughts before I can start creating a dangerously handsome image in my mind.

Dani looks at me with a grin, and I pull her into a tight hug. "I'm so happy for you, and I love you so much. I promise I'll try to keep it together."

She pulls back, her gaze warm. "Puddle away, my beautiful friend. I love you too."

"Hey, save that kind of talk for your future husband!" Stella teases, handing Dani her bouquet.

"Oh my god – husband!" Dani squeals, her excitement filling the room.

I grab my own flowers, and we head toward the door. This is it.

I've never been a bridesmaid before, so I've never walked down the aisle. The bride is the main event, which does take the pressure off, but still, being the centre of attention in such an important moment is daunting.

Out of all the familiar faces I knew would be here, there was only one I was desperately trying not to look for – and yet could not wait to see.

As we begin to walk through the door, I catch a glimpse of the hall, beautifully adorned with white flowers and pine, elegantly decorating the lines of chairs.

I step through the doors, finally looking up from my bouquet, and there he is – Ryan.

Standing in a dark green suit, looking absolutely starstruck, mouth slightly open. A deep breath fills my lungs, and I take a careful step forward. Despite everything – the weeks apart, the hurt, the distance between us – seeing him stills something in me. It's like the world is taking a breath with me, and for a moment, everything feels a little easier.

As I move towards the altar, I realise it's not the man I'm walking toward that matters. It's the journey I'm taking toward something better, toward a truer version of myself. It's being able to make decisions and find the joy and light on my own. Every step feels like a lifetime, but in this moment, I focus on just moving forward.

It's cruel, walking down the aisle toward Ryan, knowing we're not – and won't be – together. It's almost like stepping into a daydream, one I would've shut down quickly because it hurt too much to imagine it could come true. But here I am, facing it. In some parallel universe, maybe there's a version of this day where I'm walking towards the man I love in a beautiful dress, and he's waiting for me. But not in this reality. In this one, I walk toward a man I – a man I miss. And can't be with.

When I reach the front, I tear my gaze away from Ryan and smile at Leo, who's looking past me with sunlight in his eyes. Turning, I see Dani, arm in arm with Sandra, coming down the aisle behind me.

I feel the first tear fall, but I don't care. The sight of her pulls me back to the present, to the joy of standing with the friends I love, sharing in their beautiful moments. Puddles and all.

Chapter 26. Him.

Never have I cried so much in one day. Or even one hour. The emotional turmoil with Anna may have compounded it, but the ceremony was beautiful. Dani and Leo did their own vows which had everyone in tears, so at least I wasn't alone.

I tried not to look at Anna too much, but it was difficult. Watching her walk down the aisle I felt my heart stop. She looked absolutely beautiful. Her hair in soft waves, pulled back on one side to reveal her collarbone and shoulders. It feels like years since I've seen her.

Every time I glanced over at her during the ceremony tears were falling silently down her face and she looked absolutely enraptured by her two friends standing together.

I knew she was giving a speech so, despite everyone muscle in my body aching to talk to her, I kept my distance. I didn't want to distract her. Which felt like a great plan until now, because despite being unable to keep my eyes off her all day, I now can't find her.

We've just finished dinner and they're starting to clear the plates, everyone milling around having drinks while they set up the dance floor.

I can't see anyone I recognise who may know where Anna is, except Leo who is chatting to his parents. I'm not going to interrupt that for my sake, so I'll have to do this the old-fashioned way. I'm going on an adventure.

Heading out of the ballroom I start towards the courtyard. Despite having the past few hours to think about it, I have no idea what I want to say – or where to go. I'm pretty sure that the bridal suite is on the other side of the building, so I start to head in that direction, maybe she and Dani went back for a break from socialising? My cool has started to slip as my calm walk takes on a nervous pace.

Stumbling through the gardens, I'm greeted by a crowd of excited friends and family standing with their drinks. Those nearest to me are fully absorbed in drinking and talking, no appreciation for the potential imminent crisis.

This has nothing to do with the bride and groom, but still feels like it warrants crisis level status to me.

Straightening my jacket, I force a reassuring smile and walk purposefully toward the doors on the far side. As I step inside, I'm met with a line of identical blue doors. This feels like the worst escape room ever. I need a button to press for a clue before time runs out. Just as I'm about to start knocking on each door, I pause.

What if she doesn't want to go out with me now? What if Leo was wrong and she never did? Am I being arrogant for even considering asking her out after she specifically told me she didn't want to keep seeing me?

This whole casual-friend-date situation has completely thrown me, and it's all my fault. I've been so focused on navigating these self-imposed lines between casual and serious that I've tied myself in knots.

"Ryan?"

A voice behind me breaks my spiralling thoughts. I turn to see May stepping out of one of the doors, wearing a long red dress. I'm not normally one to follow red flags but this is the perfect clue to guide me.

"Are you okay?" she asks, concern evident in her eyes.

"Yep, everything's fine. Sorry, I just need to go in there." I say, gesturing at the door behind her.

"The ladies' bathroom?"

"Uh, no, sorry." Okay, not the perfect clue, but at least it narrows down my options. "Do you know where the bridal suite is?"

May crosses her arms and frowns. "Why?"

"I need to speak to Anna." I try to keep my tone calm and friendly, but the urgency is building inside.

May studies me for a moment without responding. I don't mean to be pushy, but if she doesn't say something soon, I might have to abandon all dignity and start banging on doors regardless of whether she keeps staring at me. Just as panic starts to set in, she stands a little taller, as if steeling herself.

"You seem like a perfectly nice guy, Ryan, and you're Leo's best friend, so I'm going to hope you have a good heart, too," she begins, locking eyes with me.

"I'll tell you where the bridal suite is, but first, I need to say something. If you're going to tell Anna that you miss her and want to hook up as if it's some fun meaningless fling, or if you're still not quite sure what you want, please don't. Do the kind thing and just leave her alone. She may seem cool and collected like she doesn't care, but…" May trails off, searching for the right words.

"But she does care," I finish for her. "I know. She cares so much, maybe too much, about almost everything. Like her job, or how to decorate a pub for a party, or what makes a great baked cheesecake, or whether *Dredd* is a good pick-me-up movie. I could easily list a hundred things Anna cares about because she finds new things to love every day."

May smiles for a moment before refocusing her gaze, still intent on me.

"Exactly. You're both adults, and you can make your own choices. But I had to say this because I love her. I hope, as a nice guy with a good heart, you wouldn't do anything that might hurt her, unless you're sure," she insists, her gaze unwavering.

"I'm sure," I reply, her words echoing in my mind – *just leave her alone*.

But I don't want something meaningless. If anything, this conversation reminds me how much I truly miss her. I have to tell Anna how I feel and that I want something real.

May relaxes her gaze, though scepticism lingers in her eyes. "I hope you mean it. The bridal suite is the last door on the left."

Not giving myself another second to think, and with no idea what I'm going to say, I knock on the door. Inside, I can hear excited voices, music, and laughter.

Stella opens the door. She looks surprised for a moment, then slightly pleased. "Hey, Ryan! Is everything okay?"

"Is Anna there?" I ask, trying to steady my breathing, which is embarrassingly fast after such a short run down the corridor. I can't help but think again, what if she doesn't want to see me? What if I've messed things up too badly? But I have to try.

"Anna, you've got a visitor!" Stella calls, stepping back and leaving me waiting outside. I start pacing nervously in the hall, the whispers inside heightening my anxiety.

What if she's already made up her mind?

I think back to the first time she stayed at mine, waking up with her in my arms. The memory of the warmth of her soft skin against my chest, her hand resting lightly on my side, fills me with a sense of peace. I remember gently running my fingers down her back, burying my face in her hair, inhaling the scent that felt like home. Every morning together since then has felt like a secret garden – a beautiful, private space where we could be completely ourselves, away from the outside world. But I don't want it to remain a secret anymore. She deserves to know just how much she means to me.

After a few moments, the door reopens, and I look up to see Anna standing in the doorway. She looks stunning. She's holding a stray flower from her bouquet, the soft white petals twirling between her slender fingers. Her dark blue dress flows as if a gentle breeze is passing through the hall, even though everything else is still.

The sight of her standing in front of me reminds me just how much I've missed her. But as I register her confused and nervous expression, I pull myself together.

"Hey," I say, my voice steady despite the flutter in my chest.

"Hi," she replies after a brief pause. "Erm…what's up?"

She looks genuinely uncomfortable, standing incredibly still like she's locked into place, her fingers fidgeting with the rings on her hand. She seemed fine every time I saw her today, so cool and collected. Suddenly she's come undone.

This is it. I just have to be brave. I need to get to the point.

"So, I know I'm months too late, but I don't want to stop what we had. Actually, I do want to stop that, but only because I want more. I want to spend real time with you – movie nights, and quiet moments, and coffee shops, and museums and anything else. Your text ending things took me by surprise, and I was really hurt. I didn't know what to say. But what I do know is I want to be with you. And I realise this is on me, I'm the one who let us slip into this mess. But if you're open to it, I'd love to take you on a proper date." I say, pouring my heart out. She looks at me blankly.

"Because I really like you," I add, wanting to make sure my feelings are clear.

Why isn't she responding?

She continues to stare at me, expressionless. I glance towards the background chatter from the hall, which is getting progressively louder as the dance floor is almost ready. We both stand for a moment, and I try again.

"So, what do you think? Do you want to go out with me?" I ask, feeling almost childish but not sure how to be any clearer.

She looks away, her gaze dropping to the floor as she fiddles nervously with her rings, threading the flower stem through her fingers. I don't know what else to say. I don't understand what's happening, but I can't stand the fact I'm making her feel this way. I just want her to know how much I care.

"Or I can…come back?" I say uncertainly after another pause.

"Um, maybe. Sorry," she replies, sounding flustered. "I just…I can't think about it right now. My mind is blank. I'm sorry. Can you give me a minute to think?" She meets my gaze again, searching for something, her vulnerability evident.

It's not the answer I hoped for, but seeing the stress on her face makes me want to protect her from it in any way I can. I take a step back, trying to create space. "Of course, no rush. Enjoy the day. I'll see you later."

She looks a bit relieved, but there's a glimmer of tears in her eyes. I long to hold her, but I know now isn't the right time. I feel terrible for making her look this way, but there's nothing more I can say. I start to walk away.

"Thanks Ryan," she breathes out, "I'll see you later."

Just before I turn away, I add, "You look beautiful, by the way."

Then I walk off, wishing things had gone differently.

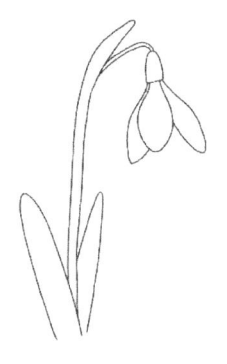

Chapter 27. Her.

Closing the door behind me, I feel the tears starting to fall. In an instant, Dani and Stella rush over, wrapping their arms around me in a comforting embrace, their concern palpable.

"No, no, I'm fine," I insist, trying to bat them away. "This is so not about me."

"Hey, Anna, I'm actually fine. In fact I'm having the best day of my life, even though you're crying – no offence. So just tell us what happened," Dani says. She's been so relaxed and content all day. No wonder she isn't stressed even now, with her Maid of Honour crying over her own personal drama.

Looking up at her, I see the warmth in her smile, full of love and support. It's almost unbearable to be loved this much. She pulls me into a tight hug, holding me until my tears begin to subside. The quiet of the bridal suite is a welcome escape from the noise of guests outside.

After a few moments, I step back, take a deep breath, and

finally say, "Ryan wants to ask me out on a date. He says he really likes me." The room buzzes with excitement.

"That's amazing!" Stella exclaims, her face lighting up with joy.

"Why do you sound like it's the end of the world?" Dani asks, tilting her head in confusion.

"Because I don't believe him," I reply, the words tumbling out before I can catch them. If I had been calmer, I might have chosen my words more carefully. But the truth is, I can't wrap my head around the idea that he genuinely likes me. It feels like a lie or that he has some other motive.

Dani's expression softens. "Anna, why would he say it if he didn't mean it? You're incredible; he'd be lucky to be with you. He's smart, and he's realised that," she says, with Stella nodding in agreement.

I glance down at my rings, spinning one around nervously as I untangle the flower stem. I want to believe them, and Ryan, but it feels too frightening after so many times of being hurt.

"Look at me," Dani says firmly, lifting my chin so I have to meet her gaze. "You are kind, smart, beautiful, and an amazing friend. I wish you could see yourself the way we do, or the way you see any of us. If you did, you'd understand why it makes sense for him to like you. I know you've dated unreliable people in the past, but Ryan isn't like that. He wouldn't say something he didn't mean. He likes you. When he looks at you, you can just tell."

Before I can respond, the door opens again, and Sandra peeks in, announcing that it's time for the first dance. Dani glances back at me, gently wiping the tears from my face.

"Just take a breath and think about it. I really believe this could be something good," she says.

"Thank you," I reply, my voice a little shaky. "I'm sorry for crying."

"Come on, you don't need to apologise," Dani says, holding my hands for a moment before stepping forward to head back to the hall.

"And you can always pass them off as tears of joy," Stella adds with a warm smile, lightly holding my hand as we start to walk together.

Stepping back into the hall it's been transformed to make space for a dance floor centre stage, tables pushed to the side to provide seats for those not brave enough to dance or wanting a break.

Dani walks over to Leo and they smile at each other as Etta James starts to play and they move together, absolutely glowing with joy.

Ryan stands across the floor, looking so handsome it takes my breath away. It reminds me of the first time I saw him – sitting next to me in the bar, exuding warmth and calm. I was captivated by his kind eyes and the soft freckles dotting his cheeks. Ever since that first moment, I've convinced myself he couldn't possibly like me. Even as we spent more time together, I clung to that belief, reinforcing it with every action I took. The late reply to my text was the nail in the coffin of my hopes.

But maybe I was wrong. Maybe I forced him into a box he wasn't meant to be in. Maybe I should give him a chance.

This man, who has a way of lifting my spirits when I'm down, making me feel cherished every time we're together. He creates a safe haven for me just by being himself, showing me what a true relationship could be like. Could he be feeling the same way? Perhaps that missed text was a mere coincidence, not a red flag. Maybe not every amber flag needs to be painted red.

Looking at Dani, she looks absolutely radiant. After all the heartbreak and disappointments she's faced, she has finally found someone who adores and truly understands her. Someone who supports her through the big stresses and goes out of his way to ease her burden in the little moments. He makes her vegan chocolate mousse to pack for her lunches and returns to her favourite shop to buy the cups she's been dreaming about. He puts in the effort with her family and friends, nurturing connections that matter to her. He brings out the best, biggest, happiest version of herself. She deserves nothing less.

Seeing the love in their eyes, stronger and more vibrant than ever before, could it be possible for me to have this kind of love, too?

Chapter 28. Him.

I never quite understood the tradition of the first dance, but I've come to appreciate it. The real magic isn't in the couple dancing together – it's when everyone else joins in. Because for a brief moment, if you look closely, you can see the two of them let go, slipping into a private world. Surrounded by people, but somehow, they're the only two who exist in that moment.

I almost feel guilty for watching them like this, seeing them finally able to breathe without the weight of everyone's eyes on them. But it's impossible not to notice the pure, relaxed joy on Dani and Leo's faces. That love, that connection – it's so real, it almost breaks something inside me. A quiet tear escapes, and I quickly wipe it away, hoping no one saw.

Not really in the mood to dance myself, I slip into a seat next to Leo's dad. I try to focus on the conversation, nodding along as he talks about the ski season. But out of the corner of my eye, I see Anna. Moving through the dance floor toward me.

I keep my gaze fixed on Leo's dad, my words falling into place automatically, but then he pauses mid-sentence. His eyes flick to something behind me, and he stands.

"Anna! Hi!" He says, as she pulls him into a hug and then moves to hug Leo's mum. I feel slightly hurt that John and I have only ever reached handshake level, but I've learned Anna can convert anyone to a hug.

"Hi, you guys look wonderful. You must be so proud," she says with a huge smile.

"Oh yes, Dani is the best daughter we could ask for," Leo's Mum says happily.

"Do you mind if I borrow Ryan for a moment?" Anna says, her tone so cool and collected it feels like she's asking to step out for a business meeting.

"Do you mind?" she asks me.

"Of course," I reply, my heart racing as I stand to follow her out of the hall.

She seems uncertain about where she's headed, but she eventually finds a door and opens it, peering inside before looking back at me with the door ajar. "Do you mind if we talk in private?"

I step inside, and in any other situation, I would be captivated by the enormous library that surrounds us. My university never boasted such grandeur; the shelves here stretch endlessly in every direction, filled with rows of books and lined with old wooden tables. If I weren't so distracted, I might have started browsing. Instead, I turn my attention back to Anna.

The noise from the hall fades, and everything feels softer and quieter in the dim light.

"Sorry for upsetting you earlier," I say, needing to clear the air. I've felt a weight on my conscience throughout the ceremony. She shakes her head slightly.

"No, it wasn't you. What you said was…lovely," she replies, biting her lip as if searching for the right words. She leans against the bookshelf behind her, and I mirror her stance on the opposite shelf, giving her the space she seems to need.

"I find it hard to trust people sometimes," she begins, her gaze drifting down to her hands. "Not with friends, but when it comes to something romantic. I worry they'll change their minds or just leave. I know that's normal, it's life – but it's also scary. So, I convince myself it's easier to draw a line and think it will never happen, because the pain of hoping and then falling can be so…hard."

She pauses, taking a breath, glancing up at me briefly before continuing. "That's why I was okay with us being casual. It made sense to me. But then I thought maybe we could be something more. But when you were so slow to reply – maybe it sounds silly – but it felt like a sign you didn't want anything more. Those days of thinking I lost you were…agonising. I just couldn't bear the idea of liking you more and then losing you again. So, I ended it instead of telling you how I felt. It was easier to lose you than to live with the fear that I might."

Her vulnerability hangs in the air, and I can see the weight of her words reflected in her expression.

I didn't realise I had started walking toward her until I felt my hands covering hers, pausing her nervous fidgeting. She looks up at me, tears shimmering in her eyes and silently spilling down her cheeks. She is so beautiful, yet so sad and afraid. I don't know how to ease her pain, so I simply hold her hands tighter.

"You won't lose me," I say softly.

She averts her gaze, rolling her eyes faintly. "I mean, I might?"

"No," I reply, my voice firm. "You won't. If we decide not to be together, you won't lose me. You'll be part of that decision. I won't leave you. I just want to be with you."

Her eyes meet mine, and I see the hurt and fear hidden behind their grey depths. Gently, I lift my hand to her face, cradling her cheek. "I promise."

She bites her lip nervously, clearly wrestling with unspoken thoughts. Now feels like the right moment to urge her for the truth, a chance I hadn't taken before.

"What is it?" I ask, tilting my head closer to hers. "What are you thinking?"

"I just…I wish I could believe you," she confesses, more tears spilling over.

Her fear is heart-wrenching. I search for a way to soothe her panic, to shrink the enormity of it all into something manageable.

"You don't have to believe me right away. You just have to try," I say. "I can't convince you to trust me, but I can show you that you can until you do." Her expression softens a bit, as if the weight on her shoulders had lightened slightly.

"All you need to decide right now is if you want to go out with me," I add, offering my friendliest smile, trying to make this feel like a fresh start, as if the past months had never happened. "I would love to take you out, maybe for dinner, coffee, or a walk in the park. We can talk and get to know each other better. Spend time together."

A nervous smile breaks across her face, one that gently sparkles with the possibility of what lays ahead, not with the pressure of trust issues or heartbreak.

"I would love to go out with you," she says softly, still smiling. After a moment, she adds, "I've missed you so much."

My heart skips a beat. As I look down at her tear-streaked eyelashes, I can see her beginning to relax.

"I've missed you too," I reply, grinning. We were really going out. This was the second-best thing to happen today. I had to let Dani and Leo take the top spot, but it felt like this moment might just create a tie.

"Can I kiss you?" I ask, it felt like the right thing to say.

She laughs, her eyes lighting up. "Yes, please." Leaning in, I gently press my lips to hers, and it feels like a rediscovery. I move closer, my hands sliding around her waist, while hers travel up my arms and around my shoulders, fingers tangling in my hair. The rush of connection after months apart tests my self-control. I want to savour this moment, to keep it gentle.

"We can take it slow, okay?" I say, leaning back for a

breath.

She leans against the shelves of books, biting her lip thoughtfully. "What is it?" I ask, sensing her hesitation.

"I mean…yes, please, let's take it slow. And thank you – for everything. For being so sweet and patient, for listening to me, for wanting to be there for me, and for wanting to take it slow as we start dating." Her hands move to my shoulders and she tilts her head, a playful shrug accompanying her words. "But maybe not right now?"

Chapter 29. Her.

As though I flipped a switch of approval, Ryan is kissing me harder than ever before. His hands grab the material of my dress, pushing me back against the bookshelves as he moves down to kiss my neck.

I bite my lip, painfully aware of the unlocked door leading back to the party. Just as I begin to think that maybe this isn't an appropriate use of time at my best friend's wedding, Ryan's hand moves down the side of my dress and his mouth goes to my ear.

"Oh fuck" I breathe out, hearing a small satisfied noise from Ryan. I can feel him smiling out of the side of his mouth, still holding my hips firmly against the shelf.

Suddenly he puts both hands on my waist, lifting me up to sit on the ledge of the bookshelves, and stepping between my legs. Pausing to look at me for a second, he smiles. He looks so beautiful. His hair is a tousled mess, his eyes sparkling. I can feel a warmth inside me that makes my heart melt.

A second later my breath catches in my chest as he slides my dress up my thighs. He moves his hands in between my legs, over my underwear, and starts to touch me softly and teasingly.

The beauty in his face shifts into something hotter and darker as he holds my eye contact, one hand between my legs while the other tightly grips my thigh.

Looking in my eyes, he shushes me ever so slightly. Tilting his head down towards me, he says almost in a whisper, "We can only do this if you can be really, really quiet. Can you?"

Unable to breath I nod slowly, trying to focus on being quiet already.

Ryan frowns but doesn't move. His hands are sending me into a frenzy as I try to stay still and hold his gaze. Still stroking gently against my underwear, he leans slowly towards me and puts his mouth against my ear.

"What's that?" he says softly.

This bastard. I can barely breathe, let alone speak. But I can tell by his tone he won't be doing me any favours.

"I…I can…" I manage, trying to get my breathing under control. We've only just started and I'm already falling apart.

"Can what darling?" he breathes against my ear. Just feeling his lips on my skin is already making me shake. His hand is still moving slowly and gently. It's such a tease that I feel like my heart is beating out of my chest, desperate to find a way closer to Ryan.

I take a deep breath, screwing up my eyes in

concentration, and hold onto the bench under me tightly for support.

"I can be quiet," I manage in one stressed breath.

"Good," he says, moving down to kiss my neck. His fingers are still moving slowly against me, making my back arch in longing.

His hand moves up from my thigh, gently caressing my stomach and chest, sending tingles through my spine. It reaches my neck, gently but firmly holding me in place. Being forced to just stop and feel this was incredible, and driving me wild.

Ryan was clearly enjoying my struggle, because he wasn't moving any faster. He started to move his neck against mine tantalisingly slow, his stubble brushing my skin, sending shivers through my entire body.

"Ryan please…" I manage to say.

"What is it?" he whispers in my ear, the feeling absolutely intoxicating. I was finally able to be as close to him as I wanted to be. Both of us are finally letting go more than ever before. It is a high like nothing else.

"Please…" I say, barely able to speak anymore, as he keeps moving at a painstakingly slow pace.

"Please what?" he asks quietly, the smirk coming through in his tone making it even hotter. What may have started as a smug side smile felt like a full-on grin now.

"Please touch me," I beg, feeling almost panicked. I need him so badly.

He finally accepts and moves his fingers under the fabric of my underwear, letting out a moan as he feels me. I echo the sound as my head falls back against the shelves. He keeps moving slowly and gently, building the tension and making my body ache for his.

One hand still on my neck, all I could do was grab him in desperation. Unable to express how it felt in any other way, I grab his shirt with one hand, twisting the fabric between my fingers to try to bring him closer. With the other hand in my mouth, I bite down to keep quiet as promised.

When I can't handle it anymore, I finally ask for the one thing I really wanted.

"Please fuck me."

He pauses for a second. I can feel him breathing heavily against me.

"Are you sure?" he asks, still leaning against me. He plants a soft kiss against my neck, practically holding me up against the shelves as I had been writhing so much.

"Please, please yes," I beg, as it's all I can do. I want him to be as physically close as possible.

Standing back, he starts to undo his belt, staring me down. I'm still trying to control my breathing, but watching him undress isn't doing anything to help me calm down.

A moment later and he's up against me, one hand pulling my underwear to the side. His other hand is under my knee lifting my leg and pulling me closer. He starts sliding in so slowly it's like he's trying to kill me.

"Please, please, please," I beg quietly, trying to move my hips towards him. But his other hand holds me firmly in place as he keeps grinding so slowly, it's intoxicating and incredible. His face is still pressed in my neck moving against me, his stubble brushing against me as he kisses my jaw. I feel like something blinding and beautiful is burning inside me and pouring out at the seams.

When I'm almost shaking, he starts to grind in rhythm, his hands still holding me up. It feels so exquisite I can barely breathe. I hold onto his shoulders, pulling at his collar to touch his skin beneath.

"I want to ride you." I hear myself say on instinct.

Almost immediately he grabs both of my legs and picks me up, carrying me over to the table. Pausing for a second to push the books off the edge, he turns and sits down so that I can kneel over him.

Sitting facing each other I can finally see him properly. He looks even more gorgeous than before, his eyes glazed over and lips slightly parted. Moving my hands to his face, I can't help but trace his cheek bones and eyebrows with my fingers, savouring this moment between us.

Ryan looks up at me, his beautiful eyes gazing into mine as we smile softly.

The way we were together before was always delicately intimate, but this is different. Knowing I can caress him, accept how I'm feeling and express it.

I gently touch my forehead to his, my hands still on his face and hair. Slowly, I start to grind my hips against him. It's unbelievable. I want to tear his shirt just to show him how intense it feels.

Ryan lets out a low groan. One of his hands moves up to hold the back of my head against him, while the other tightens on my thigh.

Smiling to myself, I keep grinding slowly, rubbing my nose against his gently in a light tease. He moves his face up and his lips catch mine, escalating to something passionate and intense. My hands grip tighter in his hair, and I gasp and press my face against his. Unable to control myself, I start to move faster, feeling completely enrapt with him like our bodies are intertwined as one.

Feeling his hands grasping at the back of my dress I finish, feeling him finish a breath later.

Both of us pant as we hold each other, frozen in this embrace together. I can't help but smile with my eyes closed, soaking in the moment as I feel Ryan's hands loosen on me. My hands are still tangled in his hair, so I move in closer for a second and he holds me tight again.

Smiling, I finally open my eyes and take a breath, sitting back to look at him. He's smiling back at me, looking incredibly content.

His hand comes up to touch my face, gently brushing one thumb over my cheek and tucking some of my tangled hair behind my ear. Pulling my face towards him, we kiss gently, still recovering from the moments before.

Our faces still close together, he says, "I have a feeling we should go back soon, but I kind of want to stay here forever," making me laugh softly.

"Probably," I say, gently pressing my forehead against his.

As we step back outside after untangling ourselves, it feels like we've crossed into a new world – a wedding transformed. What once seemed like an aspirational dream now seems to touch a newly open part of my heart. With Ryan holding my hand, I feel the warmth from Dani and Leo wash over me, drawing me closer as we make our way to the dance floor. Tori Kelly's voice floats through the air, inviting couples and friends to sway together.

With a playful flourish, Ryan raises one arm to spin me, making me laugh as I twirl into his embrace.

I see Dani give me an excited smile and eyebrow raise around Leo's shoulder, making me laugh again as I lean into Ryan's chest.

We fall into a comfortable rhythm, my head resting against his shoulder, the steady beat of his heart calming the flutter of nerves in my heart. Being this close feels perfect, like I'm exactly where I always should to be.

The fears remain in the back of my mind, but Ryan's presence reassures me. He's right, all I can do is try. If he can understand that trust will take time, then I must try and have the courage to give it time.

He leans back to look at me, a radiant smile lighting up his face. I'm momentarily mesmerised, struck by how effortlessly beautiful he looks in this moment, the joy in his eyes making his features seem almost luminous.

It's scary, this feeling that something so special could be ours. But as I hold onto his gaze, I realise that something, and someone, so special is worth being brave for.

Epilogue. Him.

No matter where I go on holiday, nothing quite matches spending summer with my family in Germany. Bavaria is stunning year-round, but summer is my favourite time here. The trees are lush and overflowing, and the fields are painted with wildflowers. It's perfect weather for sipping wine – something crisp and cool during the day, something rich and warm at night. The hot days and balmy evenings seem to pull everyone together. And this summer feels even more special, because Anna is here too.

We've been taking things slow (more or less) these past few months, just enjoying being together, learning all the quirks and layers of each other. Being around her makes me so happy, I have to resist the urge to spend every night she's not at my place at hers. May's already made me my own Netflix profile on their account. Our friend circles overlap almost entirely, so we're making a solid effort not to morph into one of those inseparable couples.

A few weeks back, I met her family – completely nerve-wracking, the sweat was showing through my shirt before we even arrived at the restaurant. When I found out the dates of our annual family get-together in Bavaria, inviting Anna felt like the most natural thing, even if it meant a holiday together only a few months in. She was nervous at first, but we both knew it was right.

It's early July, and the days are warm enough for lounging by the lakes but cool enough for hiking in the mountains. Today, we've chosen the latter. She's game for it, which is a relief, because my family holds the firm belief that hiking is the only way to properly enjoy downtime.

It's amazing how well she fits in with everyone. Her warmth and easy kindness thawed my slightly reserved dad, and her quick, business-savvy mind won over my city-boy brother. She clicked with my mum and sister immediately, and they echoed her friendliness right back. She even managed to build a kind of unspoken rapport with my sister's husband, who doesn't speak any English.

But today, it's just the two of us out on a hike, for her as much as for me. I love my family, and this time with them is something I treasure, but I've been craving a few uninterrupted hours with Anna, a chance to truly be alone together without the sleepy haze at the end of a long day.

All week we've been trekking with my family, but I saved this route just for us. It winds through the quiet forest surrounding the house, with trees that stretch so high, they form a hushed, shaded canopy over the trail. After a long, steady climb, the path suddenly opens into a clearing that bursts with wildflowers. The view is hidden until you step out – then suddenly, you're greeted with sprawling mountains that seem to roll on forever.

We're sitting close in the grass among the flowers, both quietly absorbing the view. The sunlight settles warmly over everything, mingling with the nostalgic scent of pine, and the soft hum of distant bees. I feel wrapped in the familiarity of these hills, of the paths I've walked since I was a kid. This place always feels like home, but today, with Anna beside me, it feels like something more. Like one of those rare, perfect pockets of magic I once told her about.

Being here with her, it's definitely magic.

I shift my gaze from the misty mountain peaks to Anna, only to find her watching me, her lips slightly parted as if she were about to say something but lost the thought. There's something in her look, a softness and an intensity mixed together, like she's carrying a secret too delicate to name just yet. She blinks and gives me a small, familiar smile. It's the kind that makes her look as if she's been caught in a vulnerable moment, maybe even about to reveal something she's not ready to say.

I smile back, looping my arm around her shoulders, trying to draw her a little closer. But, to my surprise, she holds back, her expression suddenly serious as she shifts to face me.

"Is everything okay?" I ask, feeling a flicker of concern. Anna is a master at staying composed, hiding any unease beneath a bright exterior, but I've noticed over time that she's more anxious than she lets on. Usually, she leans right into me, like a sunflower growing toward the sun whenever I hold her. Pulling away…something isn't right.

Her face reflects my worry, and for a moment, she glances away before saying, "Yes – yes, everything's fine. It's incredibly beautiful here. Thank you for bringing me." Her voice is light, but I sense there's more she isn't saying.

I hold her gaze, waiting patiently with a small smile, hoping she'll go on. The quiet hum of nature surrounds us – trees rustling gently, the occasional chirp of a bird, even the soft note of her breath. The silence between us stretches, deepening the anticipation until I feel my heart start to quicken.

After a long pause, she inhales deeply, steadying herself, and says, "There's something I wanted to tell you." She looks at me with an intensity that makes my heart skip, her expression serious but soft, her eyes warm yet a bit uncertain. For a second, a thread of worry knots in my chest, but she's smiling faintly, a kind of hopeful look that immediately eases my nerves.

"Okay," I say, placing my hand over hers to still the little anxious dance her fingers have started. Under my touch, her hand relaxes, and she slides her fingers between mine, squeezing lightly.

She looks down at our hands for a moment, as if gathering her courage, then she lifts her gaze to mine. Her voice is barely above a whisper as she says, "I love you."

For an instant, everything freezes. My heart seems to stop mid-beat. Her words hang in the air, and for a moment, I feel like I might be dreaming.

"I wanted to tell you," she continues, still looking so serious, her cheeks faintly flushed. "Because it's true. You make me so happy, and you mean so much to me. But you don't have to say anything back, I know that's a lot of pressure, really – I just…I wanted you to know. I love you."

She's holding my gaze, her eyes shimmering with a raw mix of vulnerability and hope that stirs something deep within me, like she's handed me a piece of herself she's kept hidden. My heart swells with the weight of it, with how much this moment means to her – and to me.

I smile, and with a gentle squeeze of her hand, I say, "Thank you."

Her face softens as her shoulders release the tension she was holding, and she gives me a true smile, one that reaches her eyes and crinkles slightly at the corners. "You're welcome," she whispers, her voice warm with relief.

I slide my arm around her, and this time she lets herself lean fully into me, nestling against my side, tucking herself under my arm as if this were the place she was always meant to be. I press a kiss to the top of her head, and she sighs, her breaths slow and deep as she settles into my embrace.

For all the kindness and love she gives to others, it's incredible to me how hard it is for her to just be herself, to let her guard down even for a moment.

I feel her body relax further, melting into the warmth of my side, and after a few quiet moments, I pull back just enough to see her face, the soft glow in her eyes, the gentle curve of her smile. She gazes up at me, her expression one of pure happiness, a look that wraps around me like the warmest embrace.

I reach up, brushing a thumb along her cheek, cupping her face as I lean in closer. Her gaze locks with mine, and for a heartbeat, the world feels perfectly still.

"I'm in love with you, too," I say, my voice steady.

Her eyes light up, a spark of joy mixed with surprise. She lets out a little breath, and her smile grows, radiant, like sunlight breaking through clouds. She doesn't say anything – she doesn't need to. Her hand slides up to cover mine where it rests against her cheek, and she leans into my touch, closing her eyes briefly, as if to savour the moment.

We sit there in the clearing, the quiet woods surrounding us, as solid and unshakable as the love we've built. Breathing in her faint scent mixed with the wildflowers, it feels as though every moment since we met has led us here – to this place, this time. She's rooted herself into my heart, into my life, like she was always meant to be here.

Casual

Acknowledgements

When I booked a long weekend on the beach last Autumn, I intended to read and relax. Instead, I sat down on the sun lounger, and within four pages of starting to read a book, decided to write my own. What started as a laughable comment amongst friends turned into forty thousand words, written over nineteen hours on the Notes app on my phone. That was draft 1.

Writing the first draft of this book was an incredible experience, but what was even more amazing is what came after. Editing and developing this book became one of the most impactful journeys of self-reflection I've ever taken outside of a therapist's office. I hoped my holiday would help me reset my anxiety and turn me back into who I was a year ago. Sadly, or maybe for the better, that's not how it works. Instead, I discovered a new world of thoughts and ideas that have helped me not only work through my own issues, but discover new passions and sources of joy.

Before moving into my thanks, a friendly call to action. If you found the descriptions of Anna's anxiety and fears extremely relatable – I really encourage you to speak to someone. A friend, a family member, a paid professional, whoever is accessible or comfortable for you. Writing this book helped me realise I was struggling with some pretty impactful anxiety which was running wild with my wellbeing. I thought I was living in a new temporary norm, which I hoped a few days on the beach could fix. Since the first draft, I have been actively working on improving this for myself and it has made a huge difference. I know it can be hard and confusing, but even a gentle google search to better understand your symptoms could be a good place to start.

Now onto thanks and final thoughts.

I am immeasurably grateful to everyone who has helped me on this journey. For inspiring, editing, and supporting the creation of this book (and its writer) I pass on a world of thanks to Ella, Kyung, Ellie, Hattie, Meghan, Danielle, Imogen, Jamie, and Lukas. You are the strength that holds together the ship on which I stand. I could not have done this without you.

A special thanks to the many people I have dated that gave me a world of rich content to draw from. Every bad date is an opportunity for learning and growth, and potentially gain a new entertaining anecdote.

My colourful dating history meant finding ideas to put into this book was the easy part, the real challenge was deciding which bits to exclude. I didn't have time to reference when my ex said my running speed was "disappointing", or the guy who said where I lived was a "shit-hole", or the guy who wanted to go out despite having already slept with a close family member. Missing those references is probably for the best, because if I included them, I would have to explain how I went on more dates with most of those men after those comments. Maybe something for the next book...

And finally – thank you, dear reader, for taking the time to read my story. Hopefully it is an encouragement to pursue your passion projects, because you never know where they may take you.

If a single person finds joy or comfort in this book, I've done a good job.

Emma Cavendish is an English girl who enjoys piña coladas, long walks on the beach, and the slow-burn emotional buildup that leads to steamy scenes between consenting adults. When she's not writing a way to comfortably eat a girl out on a kitchen counter, she's enjoying London life – pubs, parks, and sweet treats.

Printed in Great Britain
by Amazon